HANGING QUESTION

A serial killer stalks a fishing community

CANDY DENMAN

Paperback edition published by

The Book Folks

London, 2024

ISBN 978-1-80462-253-7

www.thebookfolks.com

HANGING QUESTION is the eighth novel in a series of medical crime fiction titles featuring medical examiner Dr Callie Hughes. More information about the other seven books can be found at the end of this one.

Prologue

After one minute without oxygen, brain cells begin to die and consciousness slips away. After three, there will be lasting damage. At five minutes, death is close and at ten it is almost inevitable. Ten minutes to die, fifteen to be completely sure. The longest fifteen minutes of your life, and the shortest. But are the text books right? And how do they know for sure? The experts seem to disagree on the finer details. They always do.

As the rope tightens around the neck, it closes off the life-giving blood coming from first the carotid and then the vertebral arteries. The vertebral artery runs diagonally upwards from the second vertebra and from what I've read, if it is compressed, that will speed up the process of brain death. Experiments have apparently shown that the complete and fatal obstruction of the carotid and vertebral arteries best occurs when a ligature crosses the lower part of the mandibular angle. Check.

It is normal to grab at the rope, or at least try, to relieve the unbearable pressure on the neck and restore blood flow to the brain. It is only natural to try and live – instinctive, reflexive – even when the neural pathways don't work, coordination has gone and all one can manage are small contractions of the muscles in the arms and legs.

The beam protests but holds as the rope twists with the strange movements: fingers curling, hands twitching, knees moving up and down in slow spasms. It resembles a strange sort of dance, a *danse macabre* to the tune of creaking rope and beam.

One minute, then two pass and the spasms and movements get smaller, further apart; after five minutes, they stop altogether. There is nothing but a slight sway that lessens as the minutes slip by. The eyes are open but vacant. The tongue is out but no drool falls from the mouth, which is gaping in a final, futile, silent plea for help. This is the climax, the most intense moment of life: the final beat of the heart before death.

Ten minutes, fifteen.

And then it is certainly over.

And at last, I can smile.

Chapter 1

Callie sat up in bed, suddenly and annoyingly alert. She turned to look at the bedside clock. Five thirty. Much too early. She checked her mobile, but there were no missed calls and she wondered what on earth had woken her. Knowing that she wouldn't be able to get back to sleep, she pulled on a dressing gown and went to make herself some tea. Lady Grey with a splash of milk, always her drink of choice in the mornings. Not bothering to open the blind in the kitchen, she took her mug into the living room, opened the curtains and immediately understood why her sleep had been disturbed.

Blue lights strobed through the early morning mist surrounding the black net shops that were unique to Hastings. In the 1800s, a shortage of storage space for the fishermen who used the beach as their base had meant that their workshops, used to keep and mend equipment and hang the nets to dry, had to expand upwards and the tall, thin, windowless, timber sheds were built. Whatever the reason for their existence, they made for an eerie sight, looming up through the mist, at the best of times and even more so with the added accompaniment of the police's blue lights.

Curious, she opened the double doors onto the balcony and went out. There were two marked cars parked in the road outside and an ambulance was just pulling up behind them. The flashing lights might not have penetrated her bedroom curtains, but perhaps the noise of car doors slamming or people talking had alerted her subconscious that something was happening outside.

Callie quickly went back to her bedroom and pulled on some jeans and a dark blue sweatshirt. She had learned the lesson about attending crime scenes wearing anything you couldn't put in a hot wash, or preferably boil afterwards. So many outfits had ended up being thrown in the bin because they smelled of death or were stained by bodily fluids. Pulling her shoulder-length blonde hair into a scrunchie, and checking that she looked at least neat, she grabbed her bag, the forensic one rather than her GP case, and ran down the stairs two at a time. Bursting through the main doors, her mobile rang, as she had expected it would. Early morning emergencies with a response like this were usually a fatality or at the very least a serious injury. It might be an addict who had overdosed, or a homeless person succumbing to hypothermia; either way, she would get the call to attend sooner rather than later, so it was no surprise when she felt her phone buzz in her pocket and heard the blare of the old-fashioned ring tone she now used because it was impossible to ignore. She barely slowed down as she answered it.

"Hello? Dr Hughes here," she said, slightly out of breath and turning to see a fire engine arrive and park in the road.

"Report of a sudden death, Doctor, in one of the net shops. Not sure of the exact location–"

"It's okay, I can see where it is, thanks." She put the phone back in her pocket and nodded to a paramedic who was slowly walking back to the ambulance, indicating that he would not be needed here anymore. A death then. She threaded her way through the dark huts, reaching a group of people gathered outside one of the buildings, and put her medical bag down on the stones.

"Hi, what's the situation, Sergeant?" She was relieved to see someone she recognised was in charge; it always helped when she didn't need to waste time introducing herself and explaining her presence.

"Sudden death, Doctor, the paramedic has already pronounced." Sergeant Ewan Bracewell glanced over to where a young man was sitting on the stones, leaning against another hut. As she watched, the man leant forward and put his head in his hands. The sergeant lowered his voice as he continued to brief Callie. "He found his brother hanging in there when he came to fetch some crates for their boat."

A suicide. Callie closed her eyes for a second and shuddered, before giving herself a mental shake. She had a job to do.

"The brother called the ambulance?"

Sergeant Bracewell nodded. "Must have been a shock."

"He didn't try and cut the deceased down or anything?"

Bracewell shook his head. "Said he knew it was too late, so he came out and dialled 999. The paramedic agreed when he took a look, so they left him as is."

Callie sighed, it was never easy dealing with a suicide, but for this poor unfortunate young man to find his own brother, it was bound to be a truly terrible, life-changing event that would haunt him for as long as he lived.

She turned as the crunch of footsteps on the shingle heralded a new arrival and saw Chris Butterworth, the Chief Fire Officer, approaching the group. He was dressed in his fire-resistant turnout gear, ready for whatever he might have to face.

"Hi, Chris, let me just get in and do my bit," she said as she grabbed gloves, plastic bootees and a crime-scene suit out of her bag.

"Take your time, Doc," he replied with a small smile. "Nothing else happening this time of the morning." He turned to Bracewell for information on why they had been called.

Chapter 2

Having completed her preparations and picked up the few essential pieces of equipment she needed, Callie approached the hut door, pushing it open with her gloved hand. As she stepped into the windowless space, the door swung almost closed behind her and she stood still for a moment to let her eyes adjust to the gloom, and her nose get used to the almost-overwhelming smells of fish, diesel and faeces. The small amount of light from the door was just enough for her to be able to make out the dimensions of the place: about eight feet by six, she reckoned. Looking up, she couldn't see a ceiling, just varying shades of gloom. It felt claustrophobically small, the side walls pressing in on her. She took a deep breath and instantly regretted it, gagging on the smell. She wished she had taken the time to stick some menthol rub up her nose before entering the hut.

Once she had regained her composure, she clicked on her head torch and her phone voice-recorder app, describing the scene in front of her.

In the centre of the room, almost at touching distance from her, the legs of a man swayed gently in the movement of air her arrival had caused. A wooden bench lay on its side beneath his feet. She described the scene out loud and, with a small, sad shake of her head, stepped up to the body. Even though the paramedic had already pronounced death, Callie double-checked. Reaching up, she took hold of the man's wrist, feeling for a radial pulse. There wasn't one, as expected. Taking out her stethoscope she stood on tiptoe to try and listen to his chest. There was nothing to hear. No heartbeat or breath sounds. Unsurprising.

She recorded these facts and looked further up. She wouldn't be able to check for a carotid pulse as the rope was in the way, cutting deep into the flesh just below the man's ear. Also, to reach it she would have had to stand on the bench and she was reluctant to move anything before photographs of the scene had been taken. He was clearly dead. Focusing her light around the side of his neck, she couldn't see any scratch marks. It wasn't uncommon for suicides to change their minds, but there was no sign of that here that she could see. The pathologist would have a much better chance of finding anything like that once the body was on his autopsy table.

Callie picked up the hand closest to her and looked at the fingers – no broken nails or signs of a struggle there, either. His hand felt cool rather than cold and when she tried to flex the wrist, there was considerable resistance to the movement, telling her that rigor mortis was either just setting in, or beginning to dissipate. Given that rigidity appears approximately one to two hours after death – depending on external factors such as temperature – starting in the head and neck and progressing to the limbs over the next few hours, she felt safe saying that he had been dead more than two hours, and probably more than four. Rigor dissipates in the same way, starting at the extremities and working back to the head and neck, usually leaving the body entirely at twenty-four to thirty-six hours after death, although again, it could persist under certain conditions.

Callie tried to flex the foot and met with some resistance there, but less than at the wrist, so she thought that she could probably narrow that range still further to between four and twenty hours. With the man's skin being cool rather than cold, she suspected that rigor was just setting in rather than leaving, setting the time of death at around the shorter part of the estimate. She took a thermometer out of her pocket and checked the external temperature. It read ten degrees, cool but not freezing, and she again noted it for her voice recorder.

With a small sigh she looked up again, taking in the engorged face and protruding tongue above a tight, nylon rope, digging into the neck, transverse across the front and slanting up to the mandibular process, just below the ears. Looking about her, she could see coils of similar rope stored neatly on shelves around the walls, along with empty crates, cans of oil, tools and other equipment used to maintain a commercial fishing boat.

The rope disappeared upwards, past the first mezzanine floor that was little more than a few planks secured across some beams and up to the second. The light barely penetrated that high and Callie couldn't see what happened to the rope up there, but presumed it had been passed over a pulley or hook of some kind, because the rope came back to where it was fastened to a sturdy looking cleat on the wall about ten foot off the ground.

Sergeant Bracewell knew that Callie, and the coroner, would want the rope intact unless there was a need to cut the body down quickly in order to perform resuscitation procedures. It was clearly too late for that. The presence of the fire brigade was beginning to make sense now: someone was going to have to climb up and free the rope, along with whatever had been used to attach it. There were no stairs to the upper levels, just a series of worn, wooden slats nailed to the wall. No way was she climbing up there.

The door opened, allowing more light into the room, and Callie turned to see a masked figure similarly suited in crime scene coveralls, gloves and bootees. There was a creak of welcome as the body swayed in response to the new arrival and the movement of air he caused.

"Hi, Colin," she said, relieved to see the short, squat figure that was easily recognisable as the civilian crime scene manager, Colin Brewer. "Just finished," she added as she switched off her voice recorder. "Can we get some photographs done before we try and move anything?"

"We'll need some lights too," Brewer said and went back out to organise it. Callie took a moment, as she always did, to say a silent prayer hoping that the deceased was now, finally, at peace, before following the CSM out. She was relieved to be back in the fresh air and took a couple of deep breaths of it before walking over to where Bracewell and Butterworth were standing.

"If we could just let them record the scene first, then we'll need to move the body." She turned and spoke directly to Butterworth. "Which is where I think you will be needed," she told him. "The rope is attached to the roof, or somewhere high up, anyway. If possible, I'd like it, and everything it's attached to, recovered intact."

"Okay," he replied. "Once I get in, I'll see what the situation is. Some of these old places don't have anything safe to climb up anymore, if they ever did, in which case we'll need to bring in ladders. I'll talk to Colin."

He went over to Brewer who was talking to a crime scene suited figure clasping a compact video camera, briefing her on what she needed to do.

"I've let Mike know this is going to be a coroner's case," Bracewell told Callie. "He asked that you call him as soon as you can."

Mike Parton was the coroner's officer and Callie knew him as well as anyone did. A reserved, dignified ex-police officer, he was good with relatives and Callie had often had cause to be grateful for his delicate handling of difficult situations. Suicides were always difficult situations.

Callie nodded and looked over at the young man who was still sitting with his head in his hands, but had been joined by a slightly older man dressed in a filthy oilskin jacket and cut-down seaboots. The new arrival was standing awkwardly beside the boy, periodically patting his shoulder in a comforting way.

"Do we know anything more about the deceased?" she asked Bracewell quietly.

"Simon Porter, twenty-five." He glanced down at his notebook. "Master of the fishing boat RoseMarie. Identified by his younger brother Carl." He cleared his throat before continuing hesitantly. "Simon is, was, married, with one daughter who is two years old and, according to Carl, there's another on the way."

Callie closed her eyes, and groaned. Why on earth had he killed himself when he had such a young family? So much to look forward to...

"I've sent a couple of officers round to do the knock," Bracewell continued. "She'll probably be awake by now with a kiddie that age."

Callie was glad she wasn't the one who had to go round and tell the poor woman what had happened and that she was no longer a wife, but a widow. It was a job dreaded by everyone.

"I didn't see a note in there," she told Bracewell. "But they'll be able to do a better check once Colin's got more lights in."

They both knew that suicides didn't always leave notes behind, and sometimes it was kinder when they didn't. No one likes to be told after the event that they are the reason a person has killed themselves.

As Bracewell went over to ask Brewer to look out for a note, Callie went over to speak to the young man who had found his brother's body.

"Mr Porter? Carl?" she said, gently. "I'm very sorry for your loss. I'm the police doctor and I know it's hard, but can you tell me a little bit about your brother? About Simon?"

"He was called Si, everyone called him Si." He wiped his nose with the back of his hand and sniffed.

"I'm sorry, Si then. Was there anything worrying him?"

Carl didn't answer, just shook his head and looked away.

"He was the best," the slightly older man standing beside Carl said. "The best skipper I ever worked for, or with. He was doing well, but… fishing's a tough life." He turned away at that point, probably embarrassed for them to see him crying. Carl looked up at him and then turned back to Callie.

"Denny's right, it is hard," he told her. "But I don't think there was anything more than that." He indicated the older man who was now loudly blowing his nose on a rather grimy handkerchief. "Like Denny said, he was a good captain, a good brother, things were better than when my dad was in charge."

Whilst outwardly more together than his colleague, Carl was speaking in a monotone that suggested he was working hard to keep himself under control.

"What about your dad? Is he still around?"

"Yeah, I live with him, but he's not working anymore, that's why Si took over." Carl glanced across at Denny, who was frowning.

"He'll need to be told," Denny said.

"Yeah." Carl clearly wasn't looking forward to doing that.

"I can ask the police to—" Callie started to say but he interrupted her with a vehement shake of his head.

"No, no it's okay. I'll do it." He stood up suddenly, as if he was ready to go and face his father straight away.

Bracewell noticed and came over. "Everything all right?" he asked.

"It's fine, I need to tell my dad, that's all. He can be a bit, um, difficult, especially in the mornings."

"You want me to come too, Carl?" Denny asked.

"No, it's okay, Denny, it's better if I do it alone. You'd best be getting home, you won't be going out today, maybe not for a while. I'll keep you posted about what's happening." He turned to Bracewell. "Is it all right if I go?"

"I've got your address," the police sergeant said with a nod. "Someone will be round later, take a statement, if that's okay?"

Carl nodded and hurried away, watched by Callie, Bracewell and Denny. He paused by the net shop door as he passed it, giving it one last look before walking on with a small shake of his head.

"Poor lad," Denny said.

"Yes," Callie replied. "Will he be all right, do you think?"

Denny shrugged.

"Can't get my head round it," he said. "Why'd Si do something like that?"

"It's always hard to know, hard to understand what can have been going through his head in these circumstances," Callie told him. "What about his home life? Was everything all right there?"

"You'd need to ask Shaz, his wife. We didn't talk much about stuff like that. He loved his little girl, though. Doted on her." He fished out his hankie again and blew his nose forcefully.

Callie patted his arm and walked back towards the main group outside the net shop with Bracewell.

"I hate these sorts of jobs," the sergeant said with feeling and then, seeing the mortuary van arrive, went over to tell the officers trying to keep people away to let the van through.

Callie could see one or two people were standing around in the road. Bystanders, watching and wondering what was going on. She hoped they would be able to get everything finished and the body shifted before the bulk of the local population were up and about. She checked her watch. Six thirty, so they probably had an hour or so before staff started turning up at the sea life centre, and longer still before tourists started arriving. Time enough to clear everything tidily away. The net shop would still be sealed off, but there would be nothing left to see other than a bit of police tape.

Chris Butterworth, fully kitted up in a scene of crime suit over his turnout gear, came out of the door with the rope and attachments in his gloved hands. He pulled down his mask and Callie could see he was a bit red in the face and sweat was dripping off his forehead. It must have been hot climbing up the ladder in all those layers. A CSI was standing ready with a large evidence bag and he put it all in there. Callie went over and took a closer look.

"That's a complicated pulley. Was that how the rope was fixed to the ceiling?"

"It's a block and tackle, used to lift heavy loads. Probably been up there years, judging by the state of the screws. It's most likely from when they used to haul the nets up to dry."

Colin came out of the door and looked towards the road. Seeing Bracewell and the mortuary van driver, he beckoned them over.

"We're ready to move the body now," he said to Callie and Butterworth.

"I'll leave you to it, Colin," Callie said. "I have to go and give Mike Parton a call."

Chapter 3

It was evening, already dark, and a winter sea mist had descended once again. Callie was sitting on her balcony, well-wrapped against the chill, and clasping a mug of steaming tea. It had become a bit of a ritual to sit here in the fresh air, looking out towards the sea, thinking through everything that had happened during the day and making plans for the next. It was quiet and calming and she wondered how she had managed all those years in her old flat which had no outside space at all.

She tried to make out which net shop she had been in that morning, where the body had been found, but it was hard to tell; with only the street lights to penetrate the gloom, there was nothing to distinguish it from its neighbours. Even the police tape sealing the door couldn't be seen in the deep shadows, only the blue and white ribbon designating the wider exclusion zone remained visible but it had been torn by the wind and those wanting access or a closer look.

There was a sudden burst of laughter from The Dolphin Inn, reminding her that she was much closer to people, and life, in her new home. The isolation of her old place had been one of the main reasons she had moved. Her original plan had been to move back there once she had got over the attack that had left her feeling so vulnerable. But now she wasn't sure she would ever feel ready to go back. Sometimes it was better to have people around you, even if they were noisy, and she certainly did feel safer here, with the pub, chippy and restaurant just down the road, and there was no doubt the location was convenient.

But death seemed to have followed her to her new home. Was it better that it was suicide rather than murder? She wasn't sure there was much difference. Perhaps a suicide made her feel more sad than frightened, which was how she had felt in her last home, but she was still unsettled by it.

She picked up her mobile phone to ring her friend Kate, thinking that maybe she needed company, or alcohol, or both, but it rang before she could make the call.

"Hello, Dr Hughes speaking," she said.

"Ah, hello, Dr Hughes," a familiar voice answered. "It's Sergeant Meredith from the custody suite. I wonder if we could have the pleasure of your company this evening?"

"Of course," she replied, thinking that perhaps work was as good a remedy as any other. "What's the problem?"

"We've had two D&Ds brought in after a fight and I'd feel happier if you gave them the once-over and said whether or not they're fit to detain."

"Of course," she replied, trying not to sound too disappointed. Drunks were a pain in the neck, and not just for her. It was the police who ended up having to arrest them, for their own safety as often as not, and put up with them soiling police vehicles and the cells. But for a doctor they were a nightmare, as she had to try and work out whether their problems were simply alcohol related or if they might have a hidden head injury that needed treatment. The symptoms of concussion or a bleed on the brain were confusion, unsteadiness of gait, irritability and even aggression, so it was sometimes very hard to distinguish between them and plain drunkenness.

With a sigh, she picked up her medical bag and headed for the police station.

* * *

"What've we got?" she asked Sergeant Peter Meredith as she signed herself in to the custody suite. He was an experienced custody sergeant and, despite his slight build, well able to help when a prisoner kicked off.

"It's Jack Porter," he leant forward and spoke quietly. "His son committed suicide this morning."

"The hanging in the net shop?"

"That's right, he's – well – he's a drinker and he was in the pub and got into a ruck with one of his old crewmen."

"And they arrested him? Surely it would have been better to just calm him down and take him home after the day he's had."

"He didn't give them much choice, wouldn't calm down and even thumped PC Adeola. I've packed her off to A&E to get checked. Then the other bloke, Richard Simmons, kept having a go even when Jack Porter was in cuffs, so he had to be arrested too. Drunk as skunks the pair of them – the surprise is they were even able to stand, let alone land any punches."

He came out from behind the desk.

"I'll take you down to the cells so you can take a look and see if either of them needs to go to hospital as well or if we can safely leave them to sober up in the cells overnight."

He led her along the corridor to the cells and stopped at the first door.

"I've got Porter in here, and put Simmons as far away as I could get him." He gestured to the cell at the end of the corridor.

"Good."

"Oi! When you going to let me outta here?" A shout came from the end of the corridor and was ignored by Meredith.

Callie waited as the sergeant opened the hatch in the first cell door to check on the prisoner inside.

"He's asleep," he told her and gestured for her to look.

Porter was huddled under a blanket on the uncomfortable, thin, plastic-covered mattress. She could see the blanket rise and fall rhythmically, which – along with the thunderous snores – told her that he was breathing. "Do you want to do the other one first seeing as he is awake?"

"Please."

They walked down to the end of the corridor and the custody sergeant checked through the hatch before opening the door and entering the cell. He stood to one side as Callie followed him in.

"About bloody time!" the man sitting on the bench said as she came in. He looked to be in his fifties, but could have been younger; fishermen tended to age before their time from being out in all weathers.

"Mr Simmons, I'm Dr Hughes, here to check you are fit to be detained."

"Detained? Why? What the feck am I supposed to have done? It was all that bugger Jack's fault. Had a go at me, he did. I was just defending myself."

"That's nothing to do with me," Callie told him and pulled on a pair of latex gloves. "Now, does anywhere hurt?"

"At my age, every bloody thing hurts." He lay back and let her examine him, even though she was pretty sure by now that there was nothing wrong with the man other than a few too many drinks. He had a bruise on his jaw line and a small cut where his teeth had caught the lip, but it wasn't bleeding and he seemed able to move his mouth normally. She checked his vision and felt for bumps on his head, then went to check his hands for signs that he had fought back. That was when she discovered he only had one hand, the right one, which did indeed have bruises and scraped knuckles. The left arm ended just below the elbow.

"Lost it in an accident," he explained. "All that bastard's fault and they never paid me the proper compo. I deserved much more, but the buggers said I was partly to blame." He spat on the floor in disgust. "Bastards."

"Oi, none of that," Meredith told him. "Have some respect."

Callie tried to keep the distaste from her voice as she stood and pulled her gloves off.

"That's all fine," she told the custody sergeant. "He's fit to detain."

They left Simmons still shouting that he'd done nothing wrong and went back to the first cell. Porter was still asleep, but Meredith unlocked the cell door and entered.

"Jack!" he called out, giving the man asleep on the bench a quick shake. "Doctor's here to see you."

Jack Porter groaned and pulled the blanket round his ears.

Meredith gave him another shake. "C'mon, Jack, wakey, wakey."

"Fuck off!" he replied. "Let me sleep."

Meredith shrugged and made way for Callie to approach the prisoner.

"Mr Porter? It's Dr Hughes," she said, gently. "I've come to make sure you're okay. Can you sit up for me?"

"Can't you leave me alone?"

"I will, just as soon as I've checked you over, so why don't you sit up and let me do that?"

After a bit more grunting and groaning, Porter sat up, letting the blanket fall, and rubbed his eyes. He smelt of beer, stale cigarettes, and sweat.

"That's good," Callie said. "Now, does anywhere hurt?"

She was feeling his head as she spoke and checking to see if there was any blood anywhere, but there didn't seem to be, just a lump on the back of his head where he had presumably hit it, or been hit. Callie took a pen torch out of her bag and shone the light into his eyes.

"Geroff!" Porter flinched and swatted her hands away. "No, it doesn't hurt," he said. "Now, turn that ruddy light off and let me sleep." He turned away from her.

"In just a minute, Mr Porter. Please open your eyes and look at me."

He reluctantly did as she asked. Flashing the light into first one eye and then the other, Callie confirmed that his pupils were equal and reacting to light. "I want you to follow the light with your eyes, Mr Porter." She moved the light from one side to the other, checking that he was able to follow it and that there was no nystagmus, juddering or flickering of the eyes. Satisfied, she put the torch back and took hold of both Mr Porter's hands. "Can you squeeze my hands, please?" As she went through the process of checking for any signs of a head injury, she watched him closely. "There," she said as she finished her examination. "All done."

"Thank Christ for that."

Closing her bag with a click, she turned back to him. He was still sitting up, a vacant look on his face as he stared at the wall.

"I'm very sorry for your loss, Mr Porter," she said. "I was there this morning, after your son was found."

He looked at her for a moment, as if trying to understand what she was saying.

"He was no son of mine," he said sadly and curled up, pulling the blanket over his head and shutting down any further conversation.

Chapter 4

The next day found Callie on telephone duty in her part-time role as a GP. She had been allocated thirty patients who had used the e-consult form and were judged to need a call back from a doctor, and was working her way steadily through them. She was comfortably seated at the small desk in her own flat, laptop connected to the surgery system, and a cup of tea at her side, the upside of doing a telephone clinic. She took a sip of Lady Grey as she listened to Mr Herring give her a detailed account of his bowel problems. She didn't know why he constantly called; he never listened to any of the advice she gave him, just went off and self-medicated on expensive alternative remedies that sometimes worked and sometimes didn't. On at least one occasion, they had even made the situation worse.

So far, she had only made one appointment to physically see a patient at the surgery later that day, everyone else having been content with advice or prescriptions.

"So, Mr Herring," she responded, once the monotone account of his problems abated. "What would you like me to do?"

"Well," he replied, somewhat nonplussed. "I'm not a doctor, but I did look this particular issue up online."

Callie suppressed a groan at this news.

"And they suggested allergy testing. I mean, I know I'm allergic to wheat and dairy but, as I am still getting problems, perhaps it would tell us if there is something else I should exclude?"

Callie had tried to tell Mr Herring many times in the past that if he still had symptoms after excluding wheat and/or dairy, then perhaps they weren't the cause of his intermittent bloating and diarrhoea, but he hadn't listened.

"I could refer you for a gastroenterology opinion?" she suggested, knowing he had had more than one referral already and that nothing had been found despite extensive testing.

"I don't think it's anything they can help with– oh goodness!"

"What?" Callie asked, suddenly worried by this exclamation and the sudden banging noise that came after.

"I'm so sorry, Dr Hughes, these dreadful people have moved in next door and they play their music so loud, sometimes it's hard to hear myself think."

Callie had visited Mr Herring on several occasions and as far she could remember a rather helpful old lady, a patient at the practice herself, lived in the flat next door. Callie hadn't heard that she had died or moved away.

"I thought Mrs Caldwell lived there? Has something happened to her?"

"Mrs Caldwell? No, no, she's still there, completely gaga now of course, poor dear, but these two youngsters have moved in to help look after her. It's them that make all the noise."

"That's nice for her," Callie said soothingly. "Now, would you like a referral?"

"Only if it's for allergy testing," he replied firmly.

Callie sighed, knowing that she was going to have to refer him, even though she was pretty sure there was absolutely nothing wrong.

"Okay, I will do that, Mr Herring, but I have to warn you, that there will be quite a wait to be seen."

Saying a silent prayer for forgiveness from the overworked booking clerks, Callie sent in a referral request. Perhaps the allergy clinic would be able to convince him that he wasn't allergic to wheat or milk as well, but she doubted that they would. Once Mr Herring had made his mind up about what was wrong with him, it was incredibly difficult to convince him otherwise.

* * *

Before going to the surgery to see the telephone clinic patients whom she had asked to come in for a face-to-face consultation, Callie took a walk down to the sea to clear her head. She had always found that just looking at the sea, and occasionally paddling in it when the weather was warmer, centred and calmed her. She deliberately chose a route that didn't take her past the net shop where Simon Porter had been found, but even so, his death was still on her mind and she turned to look back at the tall, black towering shed. Next to the still taped-off door, two women were arguing. Callie realised that she had heard them shouting at each other as she walked.

Both women could have been in their fifties but had matured in very different ways. One — a tall, blousy woman, with hair dyed jet black and more than a lick of make-up on her face — wore a leopard print coat, high heels and a shocking-pink chiffon scarf. The other was a smaller, mousier figure, with her greying hair pulled back in a clip. She was wearing a beige coat and sensible shoes.

It was the bigger, black-haired woman who was shouting and waving her hands around as she did so, towering over the other in quite an aggressive way. Callie took a pace or two towards them, wondering if she should intervene.

"Don't you call me a whore," the woman in leopard print was shouting. "You've no right to be here, he was nothing to you. Nothing!"

"It's public land, last I heard," the grey-haired woman hissed in response. "You, slut! Well, you've got your just deserts now!" Then, to Callie's surprise, she spat on the ground and stalked off, head held high.

The bigger woman looked ready to run after her and continue the argument but stopped when she saw that she was being watched. "Whatcha staring at?" she shouted at Callie and then walked rapidly away to the road.

Curiouser and curiouser, Callie thought to herself. First the father and now these two women. Simon Porter's death had certainly caused some surprising reactions. She wondered whether one of the two women had been his mother. If so, in either case, they had behaved oddly – very oddly indeed.

She wondered what lay behind Jack Porter's response that Simon was 'no son of mine'. That and the argument between the two women made her think that there was a very sad story somewhere behind it all, a story that might explain why he had felt he had to kill himself. Had Simon done something so awful his own father had disowned him? And had he found he couldn't live with the guilt? What about Simon's young family? Was Jack renouncing them as well? Callie felt for them all. To lose a husband and father was sad enough, without also losing a grandfather over some silly argument. Callie hoped not, or that, at least, Simon's death would bring them together. Being a realist, Callie hoped that Sharon was close to her own parents, as she clearly couldn't rely on her dead husband's family to support her in this difficult time.

She carried on and walked past the beached fishing boats on The Stade. They looked ungainly and out of place pulled up on the pebbles, like fish out of the water, she thought as she reached the shoreline and looked back at them. Stade was a Saxon term for landing place; she had looked it up once, wondering what it meant. The sun was shining and there was hardly any wind. Although the air was still cold, there was a feeling that spring was on its way at last, a feeling that always lifted Callie's heart. She took a few deep breaths of sea air and, closing her eyes, turned her face toward the sun.

Her moment of relaxation was shattered by the loud noise of some heavy chain hitting the pebble beach, followed by an angry shout.

"Oi! Watch it. That nearly hit me!"

She turned and saw the man who had been with Carl Porter the morning before. He was gesticulating at a young lad dressed in a dirty grey hoodie, who was standing on one of the beached fishing boats, clearing the deck. The young lad just laughed and went back to his task.

Callie walked over to the man.

"Perhaps you better stand back a bit," she said with a smile.

"These youngsters," he said, shaking his head. "They rush in without thinking things through…" He stepped back, and Callie sensed that he wasn't just talking about the lad chucking a bit of chain onto the beach without checking whether anyone was standing there.

"Denny, isn't it?" she asked, trying to ignore the whiff of fish surrounding him now that he was standing closer.

"Yes," he replied. "You're the doc who was there yesterday, aren't you?"

"That's right, it was very sad. I'm so sorry for your loss."

A bunch of old, nylon ropes hit the pebbles in front of them and Callie looked up. She couldn't see the young man standing on the deck from here, but she could see the name of the boat: RoseMarie.

"That's a pretty name for the boat," she said. "Was it named after anyone?"

"The wives of the two original owners, Rose Hudson and Marie Porter."

"That's so lovely, for two families to agree to share the name like that."

"Didn't do 'em much good, they fell out in the end," Denny said before shouting to the lad on the deck. "Hose it down and clean the crates, Mikey. Put the stuff in your uncle's shed, like we arranged, then you're done."

"Aye, aye, Cap'n." The lad bent over the side of the boat and gave a mock salute as he laughed.

"Kids!" Denny said, with a shake of his head.

"I'm surprised the boat went out, under the circumstances," she said.

Denny collected the ropes and chain and stowed them in a plastic crate.

"Yea, well, I still need to earn a living and bring money in for the widow, like," he told her. "That's why I said I'd help out, but I can't do it on my own. A mate said I could take the lad – although he weren't much use, to be honest – and store kit in his shed, seeing as we…" he tailed off. "Us fishermen got to stick together in times like these." He grabbed the heavy crate and made his way up the beach towards the net shops.

Callie watched him go. Two families who had fallen out. Did that explain the two women arguing earlier? She thought it might. Rose Hudson and Marie Porter, but which was which? A sudden burst of spray caught her and she looked up to see the lad with a hose, laughing as she brushed the water off her sleeve. At least someone was happy in their work.

* * *

This time it's easier. He's drunk. He's always drunk but, to be sure, I'd laced a quarter bottle of whisky with a few drops of GHB and left it on the back doorstep of the cottage. Booze is booze to an alkie like him and I knew he wouldn't stop to ask where it came from.

It wasn't hard to get to his place from the twitten running alongside the cottages. Half the houses in Hastings Old Town are built on land that was once garden and they all have these handy little paths leading right into to their backyards. People don't realise how easy it is to break into these places.

Sure enough, the back door is unlocked and he's out cold when I go into the house. I'd made sure he'd be alone and, there he is, lying on the sofa. He looks so peaceful, as I pull the rope from my bag. I have already prepared it, making a noose at home – experience taught me that it's hard to tie a knot with gloves on. I touch him, putting the noose around his neck, and that's when I realise he is not breathing. The bastard has died already.

I stop and think about what to do. What went wrong? Perhaps I put too much of the drug in the whisky. I am so angry I smash my hand against the coffee table, sending the full ashtray flying, the glass and the whisky bottle with it. How could he do this to me? Why has he spoilt everything? This is much too easy a death for him.

I take a deep breath; I need to do this as I planned, for the others as well as me. I need them to see this as a punishment, to know what is coming to them.

I pick up the small, empty but drug-tainted whisky bottle from where it has rolled under the chair, and put it in my pocket. I pick up the glass and take it into the filthy kitchen. I wash it and then take his usual, cheap whisky bottle from the bin where he throws his empties. I worry that he might have squeezed it dry, but I see with relief that there are a few drops in the bottom and I pour them in the glass and swirl it around. I place both the glass and the bottle on the table in the living room. I leave the ashtray and the mess of ash and butts on the floor. They'll think he did it himself, I'm sure.

He's heavy as I string him up just as I had intended. A dead weight.

Looking round when I've finished, I am confident everything is as it should be. I still need them to think it's another tragic suicide. I need to buy myself time.

Chapter 5

Another early morning, and this time Callie was deeply asleep when her phone rang. She sat up and switched on her bedside light, wincing slightly as her eyes adjusted to the glare. She grabbed her phone.

Next to her, Detective Inspector Steve Miller grunted and rolled over to pick up his own phone, looking confused when he realised the noise wasn't coming from there.

"Hello? Dr Hughes here," Callie said into her own mobile, swinging her legs around and out of the bed as she listened to the voice at the other end. "Yes, okay, I'll get there as soon as I can."

She turned to Miller, who had laid back down and was rubbing his eyes. His dark brown hair was standing up in clumps and his eyes were still puffy with sleep, making him look much younger and more endearing and vulnerable than his usual tough, no-nonsense persona. If his team and the criminals could see him like this, they would think they could get away with murder, which definitely wasn't the case. Detective Inspector Steve Miller was not someone to be taken advantage of, except, perhaps, by Callie.

"Sudden death, probable suicide, father of the lad who killed himself the other day," she told him.

"That's sad." His voice was still slurred with sleep.

"Very." She quickly found some clothes to put on and headed for the bathroom. "Go back to sleep, it's only four o'clock and there's no need for both of us to have a disrupted night."

* * *

Miller had not gone back to sleep, of course. Instead he got hurriedly dressed as well, getting in her way and insisting on accompanying her to the scene. She was a little bit irritated by this protectiveness; after all, she had been getting up in the night and going alone to sudden deaths for a good few years now, but her recent stalker had changed things forever. She could never shake off the concern that she was being watched or followed and it was a testament only to her stubborn nature that she still worked at all. The whole episode had affected Detective Inspector Steve Miller, her boyfriend, just as much, if not more.

That didn't change the fact that it annoyed her when he insisted on coming along. Particularly when he acted like he was in charge, rather than her.

"What have we got?" he asked the uniformed constable standing at the door of the tiny fisherman's cottage.

"Son came back from a night out with his mates to find his father, um, hanging in the living room," the constable explained quietly, mindful of not broadcasting the situation to the many houses nearby.

"That poor lad," Callie said as she pulled on her protective suit. Where is he?"

"At a neighbour's." He pointed out a little cottage with a light burning through the net curtains of the kitchen window. "PC Adeola's with him."

Callie was glad that Abi Adeola was with Carl; she had a great way with the shocked and bereaved, as well as being good at de-escalating highly emotional situations. "You don't have to stay, Steve," she said to Miller.

He nodded. He knew he'd just be in her way in the house but, reluctant to leave the scene completely, he went and sat in his car a little further down the road.

Suited up, Callie signed in and entered the living room that opened directly off the front door. She paused there, looking around, taking in the room, checking for any sign of a note.

There was a small, rather grubby sofa and an armchair facing the television. Both had grease stains on the arms and more than the odd stain from food and drink elsewhere. There was an electric fire to one side of the sofa, two bars glowing orange; and the room was quite warm. Steep stairs led up to the bedrooms and Callie could see through to a small kitchen at the back, where dirty dishes were stacked by the sink and the cooker hadn't been cleaned in a long while, judging by the grease and debris covering it.

On a coffee table in front of the sofa there was a large bottle of supermarket own-brand whisky, empty, and a glass that had nothing but a few drops left at the bottom. Dutch courage. An ashtray had toppled off the table and strewn cigarette butts and ash across the rug. There was no sign of a note anywhere in open view.

Turning at last to the reason she had been called out, she looked at the body. Jack Porter was hanging from the banister. A rope similar to the one that she had seen on his son's body was tight around his neck and his feet were a matter of inches from the ground. If he had reached out with his right foot, he would have been able to stand on the bottom step of the stairs and taken the pressure off his neck. If he had wanted to save himself. If.

She went up to the body and felt for a pulse. There was none. She flexed the hand. No sign of rigor. She looked up and saw that his mouth was lolling open, but his tongue was not protruding. His weather-beaten face was not engorged and his eyes were almost completely closed. It looked almost as if he was asleep. Callie wished that was the case – that he had died in his sleep; it would be so much easier for his second son to understand that, rather than this.

How would Carl feel knowing that his father didn't want to stay alive for him? And what about the grandchild, and the soon-to-be-born one? They had lost both a father and a grandfather in a very short space of time. It was incomprehensible to her that he could or would have done this to them, no matter what his reasons, his demons. Perhaps nobody would ever know what they were, now that they had died along with him. She finished her examination, closed her eyes and wished Jack Porter peace, wherever he was and whatever the reason he had killed himself.

By the time she had finished and handed the scene over to the police, it was too late to go back to bed, so she went to a café for breakfast with Miller and tried not to look disapproving, or envious, of the enormous fry-up he was tucking into, making her poached egg and crushed avocado on sourdough toast look meagre.

"But delicious," she told herself firmly.

Miller looked up, making her wonder if she had said it out loud.

"My breakfast is delicious," she told him, just in case.

His face told her he wouldn't have used that description of it himself, as he forked a chunk of black pudding dripping with egg yolk and grease into his mouth. He glanced at his watch, and then at her plate. She hadn't yet made much of an inroad into her breakfast, despite declaring it delicious, while he was busy wiping the last remains off his plate with fried bread.

"I'll need to shower and change before going into work."

"You carry on," she said with a wave of her hand. "I'm not really hungry."

"If you must order green mush, I'm not surprised." He softened his words with the cheeky grin that still gave her butterflies in her stomach every time.

"I just can't get my head around both father and son killing themselves like that. My heart goes out to poor Carl."

He paused with the last morsel of buttered toast hovering close to his mouth.

"I know, it's tough," he said. And in it went. "Worrying about it doesn't change anything, though." He stood up, took a last slurp of coffee and gestured to the waitress for the bill.

"I'll get it, don't worry, you go and get ready for work. I'm on call-backs again this morning, so I can do it unwashed and in my jammies."

"Jammies? I don't believe you possess anything that could be classified as jammies, Dr Hughes." He laughed. "Not that I've seen, anyway."

He bent down and gave her a peck on the cheek.

"Pink and fluffy and covered in little teddy bears. Maybe I'll wear them tonight, especially for you," she told him, and he laughed again as he hurried out of the door.

She looked back at her breakfast and moved it around. The yolk had begun to congeal and she wasn't really hungry, so she paid the bill and walked slowly back to her flat, trying not to think of the sort of sadness and desperation that the two men must have felt to end it all as they had.

Chapter 6

The mortuary at Hastings General Hospital was situated slightly apart from the main building and inadequately screened from view by some rather sickly-looking fir trees. On the ground floor, there was a waiting area on the right and the chapel of rest on the left. Straight ahead there were lift doors that needed a pass to open. The lift only went down to the underground mortuary. Because her role of forensic physician required frequent visits there, Callie had a pass.

Walking down the long, windowless corridor that led to the office, Callie wondered why Matt Baxter, the pathologist, had asked her to come and see him. She presumed it was about Jack Porter's post-mortem that had been scheduled to be first on the list that morning, and that he had found something untoward, but what it could be, she had no idea.

She poked her head around the office door but it was empty. There was the sound of a door opening behind her and she turned to see Jim, the mortuary technician. He was a skinny, wrinkled man, old before his time due to his addiction to cigarettes. He was extremely good at his job and Callie had learned to trust his judgement as well as rely on him for gossip and news that the pathologist sometimes didn't feel happy revealing.

"Ah, Dr Hughes, you made it! Dr Baxter wants to show you something." Jim indicated the autopsy suite behind him. He seemed a little on edge – perhaps he needed a nicotine hit, she thought.

"I'll just get changed," she told him and went into the changing rooms, grabbing a set of scrubs and some clogs from the shelves by the door as she passed.

When she came out, Jim was still standing at the door.

"Come on into the parlour," he said with a melodramatic cackle, revealing his few rotten teeth, and held the door through to the autopsy suite open for her. Inside, a small hallway had storage rooms on either side and led to a short corridor and the autopsy theatre. Matt Baxter, tall, bearded and still managing to look crumpled in his scrubs, was staring at some X-rays displayed on the large computer screen. He turned as she came in.

"Oh, thanks for coming, Callie. I just wanted to get your opinion on something." He turned back to the computer screen and flicked through some images.

"Of course." She moved forward to look at the screen.

"Here," he said, as he stood back so that she could see what he was showing her. It was a close-up of Jack Porter's face. "What do you see?"

Callie shook her head. She saw nothing untoward, but then she looked closer, zooming in to check areas of the face around the eyes, the nose and mouth.

"No petechiae on the eyelids," she said. "What about when you examined him? Did he have any on the sclera?"

Callie knew that petechiae, pin-point blood spots that can be visible in areas where the skin is quite thin or translucent, are most often seen in cases of asphyxia.

"No, none," he said, "and as you reported at the scene, little sign of facial engorgement, and no protruding tongue." Matt Baxter looked more closely at the picture on the screen, as if hoping that these signs might miraculously appear. "The hyoid was intact and there was no tearing of the common carotid that I could see from the CT, but there was some cyanosis of the lips and nails."

Callie sighed. Cyanosis – the bluish discolouration of lips and nails due to inadequate oxygenation – was very common in deaths by hanging, but could also be present when death was caused by other factors, such as chronic obstructive airway disease, heart disease or even drug overdose.

In cases such as this, the coroner would probably have asked for an external examination of the body and a CT scan. If there was still uncertainty on the cause of death after that, the coroner would almost certainly ask Matt Baxter to do an invasive PM but Callie knew what he was really asking her: should he treat this as a potential criminal investigation and suggest the coroner request a second opinion from a Home Office pathologist? It wasn't an easy call to make as it would delay matters with regard to a funeral, which was always hard on relatives and would be particularly difficult in this case, being the second death in as many days.

"What percentage of deaths by hanging have any or all of these signs though?" she asked. "I thought it was pretty low. I've certainly seen deaths with only one of the features commonly associated with asphyxia."

"It's hard to say, if you take all the signs together, but cyanosis is the most common and present here. Only about thirty-five to forty percent have petechial haemorrhages, fifteen percent a protruding tongue, ten percent a fractured hyoid and four percent have tears to the common carotid, so it's quite possible that it is exactly what it seems, but… but…"

Matt had clearly been looking up the statistical frequency in anticipation of her questions.

"You can't be sure hanging was the cause of death?" She wanted to be sure she understood.

"Not a hundred percent, no." He stared at the screen, tapping his fingers on the desk as he thought. "But it still is the most likely cause."

Callie couldn't tell whether Matt was reassuring her or himself.

"When you saw him, at the scene, did you have any doubts?" he asked.

Callie thought back to that morning, only two days ago, when she had been called to the fisherman's cottage. To how peaceful Jack Porter had looked. She had attended several hangings in her career, and none of them could have been described as peaceful.

"Not at the time," she answered, "but looking back, he had his eyes closed and just looked like he'd gone to sleep."

They both thought for a moment.

"Have you got bloods back yet?" asked Callie.

"Not the full tox screen, no, but I can tell you his blood alcohol level was extremely high. Quite how impaired he would have been is hard to say, but you or I would have been out cold."

"So could he have managed to hang himself?"

"Impossible to say for sure. His liver was enlarged, supporting chronic alcohol abuse, so he might have had a high tolerance, but it's still unlikely, I would say."

"Awkward."

"Yes." Matt hesitated, then asked, "Look, am I being over-cautious? Cause of death could be alcohol poisoning, or the tox results might show he'd mixed in some drugs too and it turns out to be an OD, so either way it doesn't make much difference in the end."

"But that would beg the question of how he ended up hanging from the banister, wouldn't it?"

"Absolutely, yes." Baxter seemed relieved. "You're right. This needs to go back to the coroner, see what he wants me to do."

"I agree. Do you want me to contact the coroner's office? They'll have to let the police know too in case further forensics are needed."

"Yes, please. And thank you. I can get a preliminary report through to them today, if that helps."

"I'm sure it will, and I'm pretty sure the coroner will request a Home Office pathologist to do a second PM, just to be on the safe side."

"Er, yes, but you might want to talk to him about who does it," Matt said, shifting from one foot to the other and looking embarrassed.

"Why? I have absolutely no problem with any of the pathologists," Callie said.

"The, um, locum HO pathologist in Brighton is currently, um, Billy Iqbal."

Callie felt the air whoosh from her lungs and put a hand on the table top to steady herself.

"Is that going to be a problem?" Matt asked anxiously.

"No." But even to Callie's ears her faint and rather tremulous response belied her words. "No," she said more firmly. "Absolutely no problem at all, and when I contact the coroner, I'll make sure he knows that."

Taking a deep breath, she turned to leave the autopsy suite, aware that Matt was following closely behind as if he expected her to pass out. As she opened the door to go out into the corridor, she could see Jim was standing there as well, looking at her closely.

"For goodness' sake, stop behaving as if I'm about to have a breakdown or some kind of hissy fit," she told them, more than a little irritated. "Billy and I were once engaged, so what? We aren't now, but we are still friends and I am quite capable of having a perfectly civil working relationship with him."

She marched into the changing room and closed the door behind her, leaning against it and trying to concentrate on her breathing, giving her heart a moment to stop hammering against her chest wall.

Billy? In Brighton? A short drive away? And he hadn't even bothered to let her know? She wasn't sure if she was upset or just bloody angry.

* * *

Callie had arranged to meet her best friend Kate and they were sitting at their usual table in The Stag, close enough to the open fire that they felt warm and cosy, but not so close that one side of their body was slowly roasted.

"Did you say Billy's back?" Kate was clearly surprised.

A local solicitor, Kate was Callie's opposite in many ways. Dark-haired and voluptuous, unlike Callie, who was blonde and slim, Kate favoured colourful outfits in contrast to Callie's more elegant pastel choices. Kate often defended petty criminals in cases where Callie had helped construct the case against them. But their differences didn't matter. She had known Callie for years and had seen her through many disastrous dates, several boyfriends and one engagement.

"It turns out that he left Belfast after ending it with his, his…"

"Hussy?"

"Girlfriend," Callie corrected her, a little too forcefully. "Apparently, he's been doing a series of short locums around the country while he waits for a permanent position to come up and, before you say it, there is absolutely no reason why he should have told me what he was doing." She took a sip of wine. And then a rather larger glug.

"And he's currently covering for someone on paternity leave in Brighton?"

"So Matt told me."

"Have you tried to contact him?"

"No, not yet, so I don't know why he suddenly decided to leave Belfast."

"Perhaps it was too embarrassing to stay after your unexpected appearance there, clearly still thinking you were engaged and then finding out you'd been dumped."

"I'm not sure who dumped who," Callie corrected her. "And it's none of my business why he left, anyway."

Kate raised an eyebrow in response, clearly not convinced by her friend's feigned lack of interest.

"But the important thing is, I'm bound to see him soon, because he's been asked to do a second PM on a recent death I attended." Callie went on to explain her current concern over the fisherman's supposed suicide.

"That's a bit of a puzzle," Kate said. "Why would anyone want to make it look like he hanged himself?"

"That is indeed the question, and exactly what Steve asked me when I told him about it. Needless to say, he dismissed my concerns pretty quickly. He isn't interested in possibly prosecuting someone for interfering with a dead body, he has far more important things to worry about, like budgets and staffing levels."

"Do you think it was the other son who did it? Strung him up when he found his dad was dead? Angry because he blames him for his older brother's suicide?"

"It seems a possible explanation, doesn't it? And that's the real tragedy here – the boy left behind on his own."

"No mother or other siblings?"

"I don't know." Callie frowned. Maybe she ought to have checked that. "I'll ask Mike, the coroner's officer – he'll know."

"Makes you think, doesn't it? Poor lad." Kate looked meaningfully at Callie. "So, how did Steve take Billy's re-emergence on the scene?" she asked.

Callie looked down and played with her glass.

"Please, tell me you have told him."

"Well, not exactly. I mean, I told him a pathologist was coming from Brighton, but I didn't tell him it was Billy."

"Don't you think that tiny, little detail might be important?"

"Yes, but I didn't want to say anything in front of an office full of detectives. I'll tell him later." She cleared her throat. "Anyway, do you think I should ring Billy and talk to him before he comes over? Or just casually turn up at the PM?"

"That depends on just how casual you think you will be."

"I can be casual when I have to."

Kate smiled and looked at Callie who could feel a tell-tale flush rising up her neck to her cheeks.

"My point is made. I suggest you talk to him first. Does he know about you and Steve?"

"Well, he interrupted us in a clinch when he came to tell me he'd split with Alison, so I'm guessing he does."

"Tell me more." Kate leant forward.

"Well, Billy still had a key to the flat, I'd never got it back. I wasn't expecting him to suddenly appear. I mean, we'd split up so it's not like I was cheating on him or anything."

"You're lucky he didn't catch the pair of you in bed."

"True."

"And you think he was going to ask you to take him back before he realised that Steve had jumped into his still warm bed?"

"Perhaps, maybe, oh… I don't know." Callie dropped her head into her hands with a groan. "I don't know if I can face him. It's just so difficult to know what to do, what to say."

"I know, I know. It's enough to drive you to drink," Kate said with a smile. "Come on, knock that back and I'll get you another one while you try and find your backbone. You need to tell them, both of them, where you stand, or rather, where you lie down."

Whilst Kate was at the bar, ordering another glass of pinot grigio with one ice cube for Callie and a pint of whatever was her current favourite beer for herself, Callie reflected on what she had said.

Yes, the thought of seeing Billy again disturbed her, and yes, here she was in a pub, drinking as a result, but she was more upset by the fact that he hadn't told her that he was back in the area than the thought of seeing him again. At least, she thought that was the problem.

Their split had not been easy. Billy had taken a post in Northern Ireland, putting his career before their relationship, but she could cope with that decision. She could understand ambition. She knew that long-distance relationships were hard to maintain, especially when they were both as busy and committed to their careers as she and Billy were. But it had been his infidelity that ended the engagement. Much as she understood that he had been left on his own for weeks at a time and that, in some people's minds, most notably her mother's, she was as much at fault as Billy because she didn't move to be with her man, she still didn't think she could forgive him. And then there was Steve Miller. Had he really jumped into Billy's still warm bed? Or had she turned to him for comfort? To feel secure after the ordeal of having a homicidal stalker? Gratitude even, because Steve had been the one to save her, not Billy?

Kate came back and carefully placed their drinks on the table, and fished a couple of bags of crisps out of her pockets.

"Look, I've bought you dinner as well."

Kate really was the best friend anyone would want.

Chapter 7

Steve Miller had been remarkably relaxed about Billy coming back, or at least, he had given the impression that he was when she told him in bed later that night.

"He's probably hoping a job comes up in London eventually. His family are there, aren't they?"

"Yes, his mum and dad are both doctors in South London, although they are retiring soon, I think."

"There you go, then." And with that, he'd turned over and was soon asleep.

Unlike Callie. She lay awake for a couple of hours, mulling over the implications of Billy's return to England. Not just England – the south coast. A mere matter of an hour or so's drive from where she lived and worked. As Matt Baxter had pointed out, he would be the nearest Home Office pathologist in the event that more than a coronial post-mortem was requested. Callie was the forensic physician for the Hastings area, working closely with both the police and the coroner. Billy would know that it would only be a matter of time before they had to work together on a case, and he hadn't even had the courtesy to tell her, warn her.

After such a poor night's sleep, Callie was ill-prepared for a busy morning clinic, filled with screaming children and overwrought adults. It was with a sigh of relief that she made herself a much-needed cup of coffee at the end of it, before tackling the paperwork pile that never seemed to get smaller.

She was surprised and a little pleased to be distracted from the pile of Post-it notes beside her keyboard by a call from the reception asking for an urgent visit for Mr Herring. He was, apparently, suffering from acute anxiety.

"I know we try not to agree to home visits for him, but he sounded in a right state on the phone," the receptionist told her apologetically. "He insisted he couldn't risk coming here or going to the urgent care centre. Says he really can't leave home and talking on the telephone is difficult. I can understand that; it was hard to hear what he was saying for the noise of the TV in the background. I asked him to turn it down but he said he couldn't because people were listening in to his conversations. That's why he was so insistent that he couldn't speak to you over the phone."

Callie tried to smile and nodded her agreement to take the visit but said nothing, not wanting to kill the messenger. After all, she knew how persuasive Mr Herring could be. How else would he manage to get so many referrals for spurious illnesses he thought he had after trawling the internet for ideas? But paranoia was a new and different symptom, even for Mr Herring.

"Oh and," the receptionist added as she was leaving, "bit cheeky, but he asked if you could bring some milk as he's all out. Almond milk if possible, oat if not. At least, I think that's what he said."

* * *

Callie enjoyed walking, especially on crisp spring days like this, and once she had reached the top of The West Hill, she turned to look at the breath-taking view of the town and sea front below. With a smile, she set off towards Priory Road and the maze of streets and steps that led to the estate where Mr Herring lived. Much as she really thought that expecting your doctor to bring milk of any kind really was a step too far, Callie reluctantly complied with the request. She would just have to make it clear to him that this wasn't going to be a regular occurrence. If his anxiety really meant that he couldn't leave his flat, she would have to try and find a volunteer to help him. She stopped to buy the milk at a corner shop on her way into the housing association estate. The shop had sold out of both almond and oat milk, if they had ever stocked them, which Callie doubted, so he would have to make do with a pint of the soya variety.

Milk clutched in one hand, she walked through the gap between the large blocks of flats, built surrounding a square that rarely saw sunlight, and walked to the flight of stairs in the far corner. As she climbed up to his flat, she tried to ramp up her inner empathy. On the second floor, she turned the corner to the walkway that led to the two flats, the furthest of which was Mr Herring's home, and was surprised to see rubbish bags outside Mrs Caldwell's door, almost blocking the way. Empty cider cans and pizza boxes spilled from the badly secured black bags and Callie was startled when she tried to get past and a seagull flew up, disturbed while scavenging for food.

She quickly walked on and knocked on Mr Herring's door.

"Who is it?" he called out.

"Dr Hughes, Mr Herring. You requested a visit?"

She listened as he slid back bolts and turned locks until eventually the door opened a few inches, held by a chain, and he peered out at her. Once satisfied that she was who she said she was, he closed the door, undid the chain and opened it wide enough to let her in.

As she walked past him into the hall, he looked out and checked the walkway, before quickly closing the door, relocking, bolting it and even putting the chain on.

"That's a lot of security," she commented, nodding at the door.

"I need it. You don't know what it's like living here."

There was no doubt that he was really rattled.

"This isn't like you, Mr Herring. What's happened?"

She followed him into the small kitchen, where he quickly filled the kettle.

"Oh, I brought you this," she handed him the pint of soya milk. "Not exactly what you asked for, I'm afraid, but it's all I could get."

"Thank you, Dr Hughes. That's really kind of you." He looked as if he was about to burst into tears as he took the milk from her.

"Look, leave the tea for a minute, Mr Herring. Come and sit down and tell me what's bothering you." She went towards the kitchen door.

"Nooo!" he said in a loud and urgent whisper. "I don't use the living room anymore. They can hear everything in there, so I have to have the TV or music on so they can't hear what I'm saying. It's easier for us to talk in here."

He pulled out a small wooden chair for her and sat on the one opposite, with the well-scrubbed kitchen table between them.

"Who would want to listen to what we are saying?" she asked him as she sat down.

"Them." He nodded in the general direction of Mrs Caldwell's flat. "They can hear what I'm saying on the telephone. Everything. They listen in. I know they do."

"Does it matter if they can hear?" she asked. "I mean, why does it worry you?"

"I don't want them knowing my business," he replied. "You never know what people are going to do with the information they collect on you. I don't want them stealing my identity."

"What makes you think they want to do that?"

He didn't reply, just sat there wringing his hands and staring at the floor.

"Look, Mr Herring, tell me what's going on. Why are you so frightened?"

"It's the noise, all day and night."

"I can't hear anything now."

"Oh, they'll know that you're here, they will have seen you arrive. That's why they're quiet, but as soon as you've gone, it'll start again. The boom, boom, boom of their music. All the time. I can't sleep. I've moved into the back bedroom, my old room when Mummy was still with us, to get away from the noise, but I can still hear them!"

"Have you asked them to turn it down?"

"I tried, once, but they wouldn't listen. Told me they could do what they liked and it was nothing to do with me but I can't stand it, Dr Hughes, I can't!"

"What about getting some earplugs, or headphones?"

"I've tried, but I can still feel it. A vibration. Here." He pointed to his chest.

She could understand that and hunted for something else she could suggest before giving in to the inevitable request for medication.

"What about Mrs Caldwell, if the music is disturbing you, it must be dreadful for her, living in the same house as them."

"Oh her, she's deaf." He dismissed her with a wave of his hand. "And pretty much bedbound now, so it probably doesn't disturb her. You know how sensitive I am to everything."

Callie certainly did. Mr Herring claimed mobile phones gave him headaches, which was why he refused to have one and was one of the few people she knew who still had a landline. He also thought that the overhead electricity wires made his head fizz, and that he had multiple food allergies and sensitivities. She couldn't help thinking that he was just being over-sensitive now and the youngsters next door were nothing like as anti-social as he was making out.

"But have you spoken to her? Mrs Caldwell? Perhaps she could tell her carers to be more considerate."

"I can't. I'd have to get past them." He jabbed a finger at the flat next door.

"What about complaining to the authorities about the noise? The housing association, or even the police?"

He looked at her in horror.

"I couldn't do that! They'd know it was me!"

Callie let out a sigh.

"So what if they do?"

"I can't," he wailed.

Callie sighed.

"What would you like me to do, Mr Herring?"

"I just need something to help me keep calm, Doctor, something to help me get some rest."

Eventually Callie agreed to prescribe a very limited number of pills to help him with his anxiety. She wanted him to come into the surgery for a review in a few days, but he was adamant that he couldn't risk going out, so she agreed to another home visit.

"I'll get the pharmacy to drop off your tablets," she told him, "and I'll come back early next week to see how you are getting on. What are you doing about your shopping?"

"I can get it delivered," he assured her, as he showed her out. "I wouldn't have asked you for the milk, but the carton I had was off. That's the problem with deliveries, sometimes they give you things that are close to reaching their use-by date. I always check them when I go to the shops. Make sure everything is as fresh as possible."

She could imagine.

As she stepped out onto the landing, she could hear him setting all the locks again. She was pleased to see the rubbish bag and all the debris had disappeared from the landing. Mrs Caldwell's carers must have cleared it up.

As she got to the bottom of the staircase, she paused to listen, in case the music started up as Mr Herring said it would, but there was nothing. Other than the odd laugh, or shout from elsewhere, Mr Herring's block was silent. She could imagine that even an hour or two of music a day would be enough to disturb him, given his over-sensitive nature, and it probably wasn't as loud as he had implied. Knowing him, it could all be in his head anyway. It really wasn't a medical problem, particularly if he didn't want to report his neighbours, but his anxiety and refusal to leave his home could quickly escalate to full-blown agoraphobia if she wasn't careful. She hoped the very short course of medication would nip it in the bud. If not, she was going to have to think about a different tack, or she would end up coming to visit him every week for months, or even years, and that was definitely not something she wanted to do.

Chapter 8

Callie hoped she had timed it right and that Billy would have finished his post-mortem on Jack Porter and left by the time she got to the mortuary. But just to be sure, she called Jim, the mortuary technician, from the hospital car park as soon as she arrived.

"He left about half an hour ago," Jim told her.

"I'll be right down," she said and slipped her phone into her bag.

She jumped at a sudden knock on the window, and to her dismay, she saw that Billy was standing there, in the drizzly rain.

She wound her window down.

"I was waiting for you," he said. "I thought you might have come to the PM, but" – he turned his collar up, and shivered slightly – "can I join you, or maybe we could go for a coffee?"

"You'd better get in," she told him.

He hurried round the car and got in the passenger seat.

They sat in silence for a moment or two, both looking straight ahead.

"Well," he said. "It's nice to be back. Matt Baxter seems a good bloke."

She turned and looked at him.

"Really? Really? Is this all you have to say after you bugger off to Belfast, have an affair, and ruin both our futures? It's nice to be back?"

"I suppose 'sorry' would have been a better place to start."

"And finish."

"Ouch, well, you know, I realise that I haven't exactly covered myself in glory, but I hoped that we could at least still be friends" – he held his hand up so that she would let him finish – "or at least work together in an efficient, if distant, way."

"For us to function as colleagues, don't you think it would have been a good idea to let me know that you had taken the Brighton post? Give me some sort of warning at least? Not have to hear it from your replacement, in front of everyone?"

Jim was hardly everyone, but Billy wasn't to know who was there.

"Erm" – he squirmed in his seat – "well, yes, perhaps I should have done that. But I wasn't really sure what sort of reception I'd get."

"I've called you lots of things in the last few months, Billy Iqbal, but cowardly wasn't one of them until now."

Callie got out of the car and slammed the door, putting up an umbrella and waiting for him to get out as well, before clicking the locks and walking briskly to the mortuary door.

* * *

"I was beginning to think I needed to send out a search party," Jim said as she walked along the corridor.

"I, um, bumped into someone," she told him.

"Ah! Well, Matt's in the office with Mike Parton," he told her with a grin, clearly guessing exactly whom she had bumped into.

The office was tiny, and messier than she had ever seen it when Billy was in charge. There were files and bits of paper on every surface, and the noticeboard, which had always displayed new guidelines and memos, was mainly covered in children's drawings and photos of Matt with his wife and assorted little ones.

"Ah, Callie," Parton said, standing up and attempting to get out of the way so that she could have a seat. He was dressed, as always, in a sober grey suit and dark tie, suitable for a man who might have to speak to the recently bereaved, as his job as coroner's officer often meant he would need to do. "How are you?" he said solicitously.

She realised that he was speaking to her almost as if she was a grieving widow.

"Absolutely fine," she said, as breezily as she could, irritated that they all seemed to think she needed to be handled with care now that Billy was back. "What did the second PM show? Anything concerning?"

"Well, possibly, and Dr Iqbal is going to re-examine the first hanging as well."

"Really?" Perhaps she shouldn't have flown off the handle with Billy and given him a chance to update her. His reasons for wanting to take another look at Simon Porter's death would have been helpful, to say the least. "What did he say about Jack?" she asked Matt Baxter.

"Like me, he was concerned that Jack Porter was dead before he was hanged. There was no bruising to the soft tissue, or chafing from the rope. It was all just too neat." Matt was looking relieved that his initial instinct appeared to have been vindicated. "Plus, he agreed that the very high levels of alcohol would probably render him incapable."

"What about toxicology?" she asked.

"I rang the lab before Dr Iqbal left and they told me that there was a considerable amount of ketamine in his blood, which, along with the sky-high alcohol level, could have been lethal."

"So, he died of a drink-and-drug overdose and then someone dressed it up to look like a hanging?"

"That would seem to be the case."

"And why is Billy going to take another look at the son's death?"

"Simon Porter's toxicology results came back this morning too and they showed a high level of ketamine in his system as well as the alcohol we already knew about." Matt paused. "There was enough ketamine to almost certainly affect his ability to kill himself."

"But all the signs indicate that he at least did die of hanging?" she asked.

"Yes, but he would almost certainly have needed help to do it."

Callie let that sink in. It meant that Simon Porter had probably been murdered, because he would not have been in a condition to even consent to an assisted suicide.

"Right," she said decisively. "We need to let Steve know and get the investigation rolling."

"I'm meeting with the coroner shortly and I asked the lab to alert Detective Inspector Miller to their findings," Parton said as he looked at his watch.

Callie stood up in response.

"I need to get a move on too," she said then paused. "Do we know if there were any signs of ketamine or anything that could have contained it at either scene?" she asked Parton.

"I don't remember seeing anything, but they might not have been looking for it," he replied.

"Well, they need to look for it now," she said as they both headed back to the outside world.

* * *

Miller's office was little more than a cubicle carved out from the corner of the main, open-plan room the rest of his team used. It was a depressing space, Callie always thought, and especially today with the drizzle slowly running down the solitary and rather grubby window.

"Shit," Miller said when she told him about the post-mortem findings. "They both might have been murdered?"

"Or not," Detective Sergeant Bob Jeffries chipped in. "I mean, they were tough blokes, they could have high resistance to drugs and alcohol."

"But Jack Porter couldn't have hanged himself after death."

"Couldn't he have done it just as he was dying?" Jeffries continued to play devil's advocate. "You know, had the rope round his neck ready and then passed out?"

"It's possible, I suppose, but I think we have to assume they were both murdered, or, at least, helped to die and that's still a crime." Callie wasn't going to let him delay the investigation. "Was any ketamine found at either scene? Was either man known to have been a drug user?"

"Dunno. But anyway—"

Miller held up his hand to stop Jeffries arguing further.

"I take it Mike Parton will be briefing the coroner, and he's going to ask us to investigate either way, so there's no point arguing, Bob," he said to his sergeant before turning back to Callie. "I'll get onto forensics, get them to check everything and report back ASAP."

"Thank you," Callie smiled and gave him a little nod.

Jeffries scowled. He knew what was coming next.

"Bob, can you get the team together for a briefing? I'll go and speak to the super, see how he wants to play this."

"Rather you than me," Jeffries said, with a shake of his head. "He's not going to be happy about his budget," he added as an aside to Callie as he left.

* * *

I have to assume that suspicions have been raised by now. They might have found the drugs in their blood or realised that bastard Jack died before I could hang him, before I could tell him why or he even understood what was happening. I won't get away with a third suicide. Not now. Not when the victims are all connected. The family must be beginning to wonder if they are cursed or something by now. I like that. I like that I am frightening them, at least I hope I am, but I'll have to be more careful, plan things better in case they are on their guard. Not all of the culprits are alcoholics and the ones that aren't won't make it easy for me. I'd still like to hang them all, though. It sends a message: guilty of murder. Because they are. All of them. And they deserve capital punishment for it. It's just a shame I can't punish the main offender. The one who I blame the most. It's a pity he's already dead.

Chapter 9

Knowing that Miller would have the investigation into the two deaths up and running as soon as possible, Callie returned to the surgery. She wanted to find out more about the father and son, now that she believed them to have been killed. Bob Jeffries might be clutching at straws, hoping that the science was wrong and these were not cases for the police, but Callie was convinced. Whatever else he might be, Billy was a very good pathologist.

She had already checked whether or not either of the dead men were patients at her practice, and discovered that they were. At that time, she was simply looking to see if there were any indicators that either had been suicidal and whether any opportunities to prevent their deaths had been missed. She had been relieved to discover there was nothing in their past medical histories to tell her anything much at all. Jack had been given smoking and alcohol advice when he last came into the surgery with a chest infection several years earlier, but Simon hadn't been seen in a decade.

Now, she wanted to look at next-of-kin data, to find someone who would be able to tell her more about the family and why father and son had been killed. Jack had listed a wife, Marie, as his next of kin, which was strange as she had seen no sign of a woman living where he had died. A brief look at the register revealed that there was no Marie Porter listed as a patient, so perhaps she had moved away and he was separated or divorced but had never updated his records. It wasn't an uncommon problem. Simon's next of kin was listed as Sharon Porter, his wife; Callie made a note of the address. Sharon's record was much more up to date, with contraceptive advice, well-woman checks and later, details of her pregnancies. Callie wondered how she was coping; she picked up the phone to call the community midwife listed for Sharon and was lucky to find her free and able to talk.

"That poor woman," the midwife said as soon as Callie told her who she was ringing about. "I went to see her yesterday and she was in a right state, couldn't get her head around why he killed himself."

Callie refrained from correcting her. There would be time enough for the fact that Simon Porter had been murdered to come out and she certainly didn't want the midwife to know before the family.

"And you know Simon's father has also died?" Callie said, deliberately vague about how he had died.

"No! That's terrible!" she sounded genuinely shocked.

"I was thinking I might go and visit her, just to make sure she's okay. Is she still at the family home?" Callie asked, innocently.

"Yes, well, she was yesterday when I went to see her. Thank goodness she has good friends and family support. There was a friend of her husband's there when I arrived and she said her mum was on her way to help out, too."

Callie thanked the woman for her help, gathered up her things and set off for Sharon Porter's home before she could change her mind. Miller wouldn't like her sticking her nose in, but Sharon was a patient, so it was only right that someone called in on her, Callie told herself. She would just have to be very careful she didn't tell the poor woman her husband was now being considered a murder victim rather than a suicide before Miller had the chance to, because that would really upset him; but it was tempting because seeing her reaction to the news could be informative.

The council house was only a short distance away, so Callie walked there. The semi-detached house looked a little tired and in need of a fresh lick of paint, but there was a neat front lawn with flower beds either side. A pushchair was parked in front of the drab front door and Callie had to step round it to ring the doorbell. She tried to rehearse what she would say while she waited. It wasn't long before the door was opened by a woman in her forties, dressed in jeans and with a toddler on her hip. Callie assumed she was Sharon's mother.

"Hello, I'm Dr Hughes, Sharon's doctor. I just called round to see—"

"Come in, come in, Doctor." The woman cut her off and ushered Callie inside. "Shaz, doctor's here!" she called up the stairs.

Callie went into the living room, catching sight of PC Abi Adeola in plain clothes coming in from the kitchen with a tray of tea which she put on the table.

"Hi Callie," Abi said. "I'll just fetch another cup." She disappeared back into the kitchen.

Callie could hear that the woman who had answered the door was still in the hallway carrying on a shouted conversation with someone, presumably Sharon, so she followed Abi into the kitchen.

"Are you here as FLO?" she asked, slightly surprised. Family liaison officers were unusual in suicide cases, but perhaps the case had already been upgraded.

"Yup," Abi answered as she poured hot water into a mug. "The boss was here earlier and told the family Simon's death was being investigated as suspicious."

Callie was relieved; she wouldn't have to be too careful about what she said now that the cat was out of the bag, but felt disappointed not to have been there at the time.

"Sorry, Doctor," the woman called from the hall. "Can you go upstairs and talk to Shaz? She doesn't feel well enough to come down."

"Of course," Callie called back and picked up the tea Abi had just made. "Which is Sharon's?" she asked the constable, and having been given another mug, she went upstairs.

Sharon was in the main bedroom, lying on a king-sized bed. Callie couldn't make out much more because the curtains were pulled shut and the room was only dimly lit.

"I've brought you a cup of tea," Callie said as she approached and Sharon pulled herself up into a sitting position and turned on the bedside light.

"Thanks, Doctor." She took the mug and placed it on the small side table. "I've just been trying to rest."

"Which is good," Callie said. "You need as much rest as you can get."

There were no chairs in the room, nor even a space where one could fit, so she sat on the edge of the bed. "I understand the police have already been here to let you know that they have changed their opinion about how your husband, Simon, might have died."

"I knew he wouldn't have killed himself. I told the police that. I mean, why would he? He was well made up about the baby being a girl and looking forward to it. We were so happy."

She sobbed the last bit out and Callie put her arms round the poor woman and stroked her back, making consoling, "there, there" noises.

At last Sharon stopped crying and sat back again.

"Thank you, Doctor. I'm okay now."

"It must be hard, thinking that someone might have killed him."

"Not as hard as thinking he might have killed himself."

"No, I can understand that." Callie wondered how she could get onto the subject of why anyone would want to kill the man, but Sharon started telling her before she could ask.

"I don't know who he could've upset enough to make them kill him, though. Jack I can understand – he was a difficult bugger – but Simon?" she shook her head. "Everyone liked him."

Callie stayed with her for a while longer but she seemed mystified at who could have done it. Before she left, Callie remembered to ask a few questions about the pregnancy, confirm when the due date was, check her patient's blood pressure and look for signs of ankle swelling. She was supposed to be there in her capacity as a doctor, after all.

Back in the living room, Abi was drinking tea and checking her phone. "Shaz's mum's taken the little one to the park," she said by way of explanation.

"And I don't suppose she has any idea about who could have done this either?" Callie asked.

"Nope, everyone loved Simon Porter, apparently."

"Apparently being the operative word," Callie said.

She took her leave, having learned nothing of any use.

Chapter 10

At last, it was the weekend and for once, Callie wasn't on call at the out-of-hours unit. Grabbing the chance to get away, Callie and Miller were staying in a lovely old pub in East Dean called The Tiger Inn. Callie liked the atmosphere of history that enveloped her from the moment she went inside. It wasn't just the beams and the open fire, it was the story about how the pub had got its name that she loved. Apparently, in the fifteenth century, the local landowner's coat of arms had featured a leopard rampant, but the people living in the village mistook the animal for a tiger and the pub was named after it. An understandable mistake as none of them were likely to have ever seen either a tiger or a leopard in the flesh back then.

The pub was comfortable, warm and at walking distance from Beachy Head if they wanted to venture out, always supposing the rain ever stopped.

They had stayed in the village before because Miller liked the pub too. It served good beer and hearty food and it was a long way out of Hastings, so he wasn't likely to bump into anyone he'd arrested. It meant he could relax, and Callie understood the feeling; she was forever bumping into patients in the supermarket or her local pub, and it could be embarrassing when they asked about test results or wanted to show her something they were worried about.

The plan was to arrive in time for lunch on the Saturday and leave again after lunch on Sunday. Just one night away, but a mini-break that was a world away from their respective workloads and problems. It was supposed to be a time when they could concentrate on each other. Callie had promised herself that she wouldn't bring up the current investigation into the two deaths or Billy's involvement; in fact she wouldn't even think about them or him. She wanted to forget about all of it and just chill out and enjoy herself.

After a wet drive from Hastings, they checked in to their room, looked out of the window and decided to have lunch and see if the rain stopped. It didn't. The rain wasn't heavy, but Callie knew from past experience that the wind on Beachy Head was formidable and even light drizzle could be highly unpleasant when it came at you from a horizontal angle. So they went up to their comfortable room and spent the afternoon in bed. Bliss.

They were having dinner – seabass for Callie and bangers and mash for Miller – when things began to go downhill.

Callie was wondering if she would have room for a dessert. She always used to have one when she went out for dinner with Billy, in the days when they were together, but Miller wasn't one for puddings, and so, not wanting to be the only one eating – it made her feel greedy – she usually gave in and skipped it. But this time, she'd spotted chocolate orange torte on the menu and was wondering if she could tempt him to share it with her. Billy would have agreed in a heartbeat and probably asked for extra ice-cream to go with it. She smiled at the thought. Both Billy and Miller loved their food, but she had more in common with Billy's choices.

"Penny for them," Miller said, startling Callie, and she couldn't help a slight flush of guilt for thinking about Billy. She had always thought that it was very dangerous to ask someone what they were thinking about and she was tempted to tell Miller so.

"Just thinking about having a pudding," she said, which wasn't exactly untrue.

"And it makes you smile?"

"Sometimes, yes. Not all puddings of course, but crème brûlée and profiteroles and, in this instance, chocolate orange torte."

"But you never eat them. Always worrying about your weight or something."

"No, it's because I rarely get the chance to have them," she corrected him, trying not to sound tetchy and failing.

Any mention of her weight irritated her, even though she was naturally quite slim. Her stick-thin mother was always on about it, telling Callie that she was watching her weight because she didn't want to get fat and giving her daughter meaningful looks. Or asking if Callie had put on a couple of pounds and then ostentatiously refusing to eat potatoes, bread or anything sweet, and making Callie feel guilty if she didn't follow suit.

"You can have one. Of course, you can. I don't mind. I can have a coffee, or cheese and biscuits or something." He stood to go and order it for her.

"No, no, it's okay, I'm not sure I have room for one now, it was just a thought."

He hesitated, unsure what he should do next. To order a torte or not to order it?

"I'll get some more drinks," he finally said and went to the bar, where she could hear him ordering her a torte despite her saying she didn't want one now, which irritated her even more. She knew she was being unreasonable but just couldn't help it.

She forced herself to say 'thank you' when he came back and put a drink in front of her, but she couldn't keep the irritation out of her voice. Desperate to change the subject away from food, and her completely irrational irritation, she broke her promise to herself and asked about the case.

"Have you been given extra funds for the two suspicious deaths?"

"I haven't asked for it," he said.

"Why ever not?" she asked.

He paused as a large slice of torte was put in front of Callie and a cup of black coffee in front of him. It irritated her further that he hadn't done as he'd said he would and ordered cheese and biscuits for himself, so she was left eating on her own.

"Well, because there doesn't seem to be any certainty about whether or not either of them is an unlawful killing." Miller was studiously avoiding eye contact with Callie.

"Billy and Matt have both expressed their doubts that these deaths could have been natural."

"I know, but the coroner said that, in his experience, when there are doubts about a hanging like this, the deaths almost always do turn out to be suicide, assisted or otherwise. He has asked for more information from the forensic team, but meanwhile–"

"But you went round and told Sharon that her husband's death was being treated as suspicious."

"Yes, but–"

"And you've put in an FLO. I saw Abi when I went to visit Sharon." Callie said this knowing that Abi would have reported her visit, so it wouldn't be news to him.

"I went round and told her because I didn't want her hearing it from anyone else." He looked meaningfully at Callie. "And having someone in the house might lead us to whoever supplied the drugs, apart from anything else. I still think this will turn out to be a lot of fuss over very little."

Callie was incensed.

"The levels of alcohol and ketamine mean it would be virtually impossible for them to have killed themselves," she said. Callie was pointing at Miller with a fork and, realising that her voice was getting louder, and shriller, she looked around to see if people were staring. Apart from the couple nearest them, who seemed to be avidly listening in to the conversation, no one seemed to have noticed. Yet.

"You yourself have pointed out in the past that tolerance of drugs and alcohol vary enormously," Miller said, keeping his tone level, trying to be the voice of reason.

"They don't vary that much," she retorted quietly, putting her fork down.

"That's just your opinion."

"And that of the two pathologists."

"*You* say that, but neither of them would commit themselves to a definitive answer. Their reports were full of 'possibly' and 'can't-rule-outs'. You know that ties my hands, Callie. I simply don't have the budget to go chasing what may well turn out to be a couple of assisted suicides. If anything does come up that changes things, we have collected evidence from the scene, we've interviewed the families, and we can always go back and review the evidence again and set up a full-scale investigation, but right now, there isn't enough to justify one."

Callie pushed her torte away, untasted. She knew he was right but that didn't make her feel better and her appetite had gone.

This was not going to be the relaxing night away from Hastings that they had both hoped for and she had only herself to blame; after all, it had been her who first brought up the topic.

Chapter 11

It was still raining the next morning, and the atmosphere in the bedroom had remained frosty overnight, so Callie told Miller she had decided to return to Hastings, making up a spurious bit of work she needed to do. Miller agreed as long as he could have breakfast first. One thing he and Billy had in common was a good appetite, Callie thought as she made do with a cup of tea in the room. It was her decision not to go down and eat, but she felt irrationally resentful at missing out on something more substantial. Especially as she had not eaten the torte from the night before, either.

They hardly spoke on the journey back, but when Miller pulled up outside Callie's block of flats, he turned to her.

"I'm sorry, Callie, but I have a hundred things on my caseload currently and I have to prioritise. You know that as well as I do."

She had to admit that she did.

"Until I am told that these cases, or at least one of them, is definitely murder, I really can't do more than a token job."

"It's not enough, Steve. And you know that too."

He nodded and looked at the rain running down the front windscreen and thought for a while, before coming up with a compromise.

"Look, why don't you review what we have now and see if you can come up with anything that will enable me to convince the superintendent or the coroner that there needs to be a more active investigation?"

"I get to see everything?"

"Sure," he said with a small, reluctant, shrug. "I don't see why not."

She smiled.

"No cheating and holding anything back?"

"No cheating, scout's honour. You never know, you might be able to suggest areas where I could take a closer look without having to commit too much manpower."

Which was how Callie ended up spending a wet Sunday afternoon sitting in Miller's office at the police station, going through the electronic files on the two deaths.

"I'm trying to get my head around who is connected to whom," she told Miller when he brought her a cup of coffee. She noticed that it wasn't the instant rubbish that was kept in the tiny kitchenette next to the toilets, but a takeaway cup fresh from a local coffee shop, which explained why he had disappeared for so long. She took the lid off the cup and breathed in the steam. As peace offerings went, it wasn't a bad one. "Thank you, that smells wonderful."

He sat down next to her and looked at the screen as she scrolled down.

"I may be a Luddite but paper files are much easier to flick through," she said.

"No arguments from me. Who are you trying to connect?" he asked.

"Well, who is a family member and who is colleague or crew and so on. Have you got a piece of paper?"

He went out to the main office and pulled one from the printer tray for her.

She drew a sort of family tree down the left side of the paper and added a another showing who worked on the RoseMarie on the right, with Jack, Simon and Carl Porter in the middle, as they were connected to both. Then she listed the various people who had been interviewed in relation to the two deaths either on the family or on the boat side, and drew lines across to show who they were connected to.

"So," she finally said as she sat back and showed Miller the schematic. "Jack Porter was married to Marie and he bought the fishing boat in partnership with a man called Harry Hudson, who was married to a woman called Rose; they called the boat the RoseMarie."

"Very touching."

"Indeed." She checked the file again. "Jack and Marie had two sons, Simon and Carl. Do we know what happened to Marie?" She remembered that the house where she had examined Jack's body didn't look as if a woman had lived there in recent history.

"Jack was divorced. Apparently Marie left him and the boys a couple of years ago. She was interviewed by uniforms when they notified her of the deaths."

Callie flipped through the file.

"Ah, yes. Lives on Bohemia Road now. Can you imagine what it must be like for her? Losing an ex-husband is bad enough, but your son as well…"

"She was pretty shocked when she was interviewed, I seem to remember, didn't really have much to say. Couldn't think of a reason why her son might have topped himself, but was less surprised by the husband."

"Well, he'd been slowly killing himself with drink for years, judging by the state of his liver."

"Quite."

"Might be worth re-interviewing her, now that she's had time to think about it."

"I don't think there are any real grounds for another interview," he said but one look at Callie told him that his response was not what she wanted. "I'll get Jayne on it, when she has the time." He wrote her name on a sticky label and attached it to the side of the screen, where there were several others, somewhat older and curling at the edges.

Callie noticed but didn't comment on the fact that he had picked a female detective sergeant to interview a grieving mother. She understood all too well the complaints of female police officers that they still got given the women and children jobs, but the fact was that, in general, they were better at them than some of their male colleagues. Like Bob Jeffries. She shuddered at the thought of him trying to be empathetic. She remembered an incident when he had reduced a heavily pregnant woman to hysteria at the suggestion she might have buried a body under her patio. No, Bob Jeffries would probably ask the poor woman if she had driven her husband to drink.

"And Simon's wife is Sharon, or Shaz." Callie turned back to the computer and scrolled through the notes from the interview with her. "We know from her interview she had no idea anything was wrong."

"No, couldn't understand why he'd done it at all."

"If he did it," she reminded him.

"If," he agreed, reluctantly.

"What about drug and alcohol use?" she asked.

"Said Simon liked a pint, but never touched drugs, not since a bit of cannabis use as a teenager."

"Has she still got an FLO with her?" Callie hoped the answer was yes.

"Not full time, but Abi is going there as much as she can, and she's got her mum staying still."

Callie flipped a page in the file. "Right," she said, "let's get on to colleagues and crew. What happened to Harry Hudson? Is he still a partner in the boat?"

"Don't know." Miller made a note to check and stuck it next to the last one.

"Because he's certainly someone who could potentially benefit, depending on whether or not Jack had a will."

"I'll get Nigel onto checking wills."

"The other person who potentially benefits would be Carl."

"Yup." Miller stuck another note on the computer.

Callie added Denny to the list of names, and said, "You've only got Denny listed as crew, other than Carl. What about past crew members?" Then she told Miller about being called in to see Jack Porter and Richard Simmons after their dust-up in the pub.

"Okay, well, if he's got a grudge, it might be worth talking to him," he said. "But you know how it is, drunks get into brawls all the time and it's usually over something and nothing."

After a glare from Callie, he sighed as he stuck another note on the computer.

"I could help with some of these interviews, if you like?" she suggested.

"No," he said firmly. "Shouldn't take more than a day or so to do these. We can manage."

But Callie knew that the chances were high that other jobs would get in the way. The interviews might take much longer to complete and there was a good chance they would never get around to doing some of them.

"Right," she said brightly. "I'll just read through the post-mortem reports and then I think I'm done."

She settled down to read the reports on the screen while Miller waited and fidgeted, then suddenly stood up, as she knew he would. He was not a patient man.

"I'll just nip out and..." He gestured vaguely at the main office.

She gave him a little wave as he went out and started idly checking what was on the desks of the other members of his team.

Once Callie knew he was engaged elsewhere, she made a note of the names and contact details of all the people she had suggested to interview. She would be able to do a bit of checking online, and maybe 'accidentally' bump into some of them if she wanted. She logged out, folded up the paper, tucked it in her bag and went out to the main office where Miller was frowning as he looked at the contents of a desk drawer. He shut the drawer sharply as she came out of his office.

"All done?" he asked her.

"Yes, thanks for that. See something embarrassing?" She nodded to the drawer he had closed so sharply.

"Hmm," he said with a grimace. "Not so much embarrassing as disgusting."

"Whose desk is that?" she asked. "No, let me guess, Bob Jeffries?"

He smiled by way of an answer as he held the door open for her, and she knew that she had hit the nail on the head. She wondered what exactly he'd found. A half-eaten bacon roll, covered in mould? A sex toy? A copy of *Misogynist Weekly* magazine? One thing was for sure, she wasn't about to take a look to find out.

Chapter 12

Callie spent Sunday evening on her laptop, looking up all the names on her list of runners and riders and getting very little in return. None of the fishermen were on social media. Sharon "Shaz" Porter was on Facebook and Instagram but there was little of interest for Callie to see there, apart from pictures of her pouting at the camera and showing off her bump, with or without her young child in tow.

Giving up on that, she tried the electoral roll and found most of the names on her list, although not Dennis Brown. There was a Rose Hudson and a Marie Porter, both still living in Hastings, but no Harry Hudson. Perhaps the Hudsons had divorced as well and he had moved away. She had taken Marie's address from the police files, but they had not contacted Rose yet, so she had no details for her. The roll only gave the first part of the postcode, so she knew which part of Hastings the woman was based in but not the actual address. Not unless she was willing to register and pay for the information, which she didn't want to do just yet. She had already established that Marie Porter wasn't one of their patients; she checked the surgery register again and neither Harry nor Rose Hudson were listed either. The Porter men – Jack, Simon and Carl – were all patients, as she knew, along with Sharon. She couldn't find a Dennis Brown there either but Richard Simmons was listed along with notes about his accident and the loss of his arm.

With a bit more browsing, she also discovered the official register of fishing vessels and spent a few minutes pacing her room before deciding that the RoseMarie was definitely under ten metres. Looking at that list, she was surprised to see that there were 340 fishing boats under ten metres in length registered as working out of Hastings. She'd heard that it had the largest beach-launched fishing fleet in the country, but she certainly hadn't seen that many on The Stade when she walked along there. Perhaps some sailed out of smaller places up the coast, or perhaps the register was out of date. There had certainly been lots of articles in the local paper about the demise of the Hastings fishing fleet and several of the boats on the beach didn't look as if they had moved in years.

She found the RoseMarie on the register easily enough, and after going further into the website, she was able to find all sorts of interesting facts about what the hull was made of and what fishing licences were held, but not much that was useful to her.

She had gone to bed feeling that she was no further on, and hoping that the morning and a new week would bring inspiration.

It didn't. What it did bring was Mr Herring, waiting at the surgery door, clutching a shopping bag.

"Morning, Mr Herring. Good to see you out and about today. Have you got an appointment?" she said as she unlocked the surgery door and headed inside.

"Er, no," he answered and followed her in. "I was hoping I could see you, as it happens."

Strictly speaking, she shouldn't have let him follow her in as the surgery wasn't open yet, but it seemed a bit too rude to just close the door on his pinched, anxious face.

The receptionist arrived, coming down from the main office to man the front desk, armed with a cup of coffee and a firm demeanour. She looked daggers at Mr Herring and was clearly about to insist he left.

"It's okay," Callie reassured her. "I'm just going to have a quick word before I start." She ushered Mr Herring towards her consulting room before the receptionist could act.

Putting her coat and bag on the couch, Callie sat down at her desk and clicked on the computer.

"What can I do for you?" she asked, although she had a pretty good idea why he had come.

"I need some more of those pills you prescribed," he told her breathlessly as he sat in the patient chair. "I know you said that you could only give me a few because I couldn't be on them for long, but they helped, they really did, and I've only got one left."

"I'm glad to hear they helped, Mr Herring. But as I explained when I prescribed them, there is a problem with me giving you more. You can get, well, reliant on them and it becomes difficult to stop taking them."

"I know that, but you've no idea just how awful my life is at the moment. The people next door don't give me a moment's peace. I'm frightened to leave the house, and the pills, well, they make my life almost tolerable. Please, Dr Hughes."

Her computer had woken up as he was speaking and Callie put in her password with a sigh.

"I will give you one more prescription, but I want you to start taking these other tablets as well. They are antidepressants and they take a little while to start working but hopefully will kick in before you finish the tranquillisers."

"I'm not depressed, Doctor, just too worried to sleep."

"These things are often linked. Look, if I were to refer you for some counselling, would that help?"

"Maybe," he hesitated for a moment. "But it's not all inside my head, Doctor, honestly."

"I know it's not, Mr Herring, all I'm trying to do is find a way to help you develop coping mechanisms that don't rely on medication."

He nodded his acceptance and she printed off a prescription and signed it.

"I definitely won't prescribe any more tranquillisers, okay?"

"Thank you, Dr Hughes, I really am grateful." He grabbed the prescription as he stood up and glanced at his watch. "Do you know what time the pharmacy opens?"

"The one by the station usually opens quite early, I think. Ask at reception, she might know more." She ushered him out and closed the door behind her. There was already someone sitting in the waiting room, a young man who looked at her hopefully as she walked to the stairs.

"I'll be back in a minute," she told him.

The patient's face fell; he knew what that meant. It could be hours before Callie came back, potentially being distracted by any number of emergencies and urgent requests.

* * *

Callie phoned Kate in a brief break between patients. "Do you fancy meeting up at lunchtime? I should be finished here about one and I feel like I've been neglecting you."

The two friends met regularly for brunch at weekends but she had missed the last two dates because she had been away with Miller, and Kate had been in London with her latest squeeze, Sam.

"Lunch?" Kate sounded surprised, as well she might; this was not their normal time to meet.

"I do eat lunch sometimes, you know."

"But it's usually a sandwich at your desk during the week."

"It's my half day and I just fancy something a bit different."

There were a few moments of silence as Kate thought about this.

"Your man not available?"

"Hmm, well, you know, sometimes I prefer female company." Callie immediately felt guilty that she wasn't being entirely truthful and rushed on. "I thought we could go for fish and chips at Maggie's."

"Maggie's? For fish and chips? Now I'm really suspicious. That isn't your usual choice of venue, or menu for that matter. What's the real reason you want to go there?"

"Well…" Callie tried to think of a reason, any reason other than the real one, but couldn't. "I know a lot of fishermen hang out there and since the social club closed it's about the only place I can go and find out more about them."

"And you can't take Steve along because…"

"Well, being a policeman might make the conversation difficult."

"Not to mention that he's probably told you not to meddle in things."

Nothing got past Kate.

"That too."

"So, it's less about missing female company and more about needing a partner in crime. Good job Maggie's fish and chips are to die for, or I would turn you down. I'll be waiting outside the surgery at just gone one."

* * *

Kate was true to her word, waiting on the pavement as Callie came out of the door.

It was only a short walk to Maggie's, a café on the first floor above the fish market in the midst of the net shops. The décor was spartan and the menu short, but pretty much everyone ordered fish and chips and plates came out of the kitchen regularly and speedily.

"Perhaps we should have ordered one between two," Callie said as she eyed up the enormous portions being carried past their table.

"I don't share my chips with anyone," Kate said, "and I could probably help you out with yours, if you struggle."

Callie looked around the room. Almost every table was taken, despite it being a weekday outside of the main tourist season. There was a mix of fishermen and locals, plus a small number of visitors, soaking up the authentic ambience.

Their plates arrived, loaded with great steaming pieces of lightly battered cod so enormous they hung over the edges of the dish on both sides, and the rest of the plate was covered in golden chips. It looked and smelled amazing, even if the thought of eating it all was daunting.

"Anything else, Doctor?" the middle-aged waitress asked. She was dressed in jeans and trainers with an apron tied round her waist and Callie recognised her as a patient but couldn't remember her name.

"Two more up, Liz," came a shout from the kitchen as two plates were placed on the serving area. Their waitress turned, helpfully giving Callie a clue as to her name.

"No, thanks, Liz, but I wouldn't mind a word later. When you have a moment."

Liz gave her a funny look and went off to deliver the food to an elderly couple sitting at the window.

"Don't look much like fishermen to me," Kate said, nodding at the people on the tables around them and diving into her food.

"I don't know, one or two of them might be." Callie realised she had better get a move if she was going to keep up with Kate. She made a start on her meal, and had to admit it was delicious. The batter was so light that she had eaten most of it by the time the lunchtime rush began to ease off and Liz was able to come back to their table.

"You wanted a word?" Liz pulled out a chair and sat down. "Oof, my feet are killing me. I'm getting too old for this."

"It keeps you fit," said Callie.

"Tell that to my varicose veins." She crossed her right leg over her left and massaged the calf, giving Callie a questioning look.

"If I wanted to find out about local fishermen, who should I speak to, Liz?"

"Depends what sort of information you want," Liz said, cautiously. "You doing a health survey or something?"

"Not exactly." Callie glared at Kate who was trying not to laugh, and failing. "It's more about the past, who worked with whom on which boats, stuff like that. Trying to see how everyone connects."

"They all do, one way or another. It's a small world." Liz stood up and stretched her back. "You want to talk to Derek, over there." She pointed to a man who was just finishing a cup of tea, his plate having been cleared. He'd been with several other men earlier, but they had all left. "If he doesn't know, his dad will, they've been working the boats for donkey's years. Oi, Derek, come over here a minute," Liz shouted.

The man took a final swig of his tea before getting up and ambling over.

"The doc here wants to know about fishermen and stuff," Liz told him and, job done, went back to the kitchen, collecting a few empty plates as she went.

Derek sat on the chair she had vacated.

"How can I help?"

He looked to be in his late thirties, but his weather-beaten face made it hard to know.

"The RoseMarie," Callie said. She had decided that it was best to just come straight out with it rather than beat about the bush.

"Terrible business," Derek said. "It's been a shock for us all." He was looking wary now. Callie's question wasn't what he had been expecting. "What's your interest in it?"

"I was the doctor who had to certify both Simon and his dad, and I suppose I'm just trying to work out why it… well, why it happened."

"Like us all, then. It's just a real mystery, like. I mean, I knew Si, had a pint with him now and then, shared a bit of banter but he never seemed like the type to, you know…"

"One thing I have learned, is that anyone can be 'the type' if they are under enough pressure."

"I suppose so. But no one I've talked to thought that he was, you know, depressed or anything. If anything, things were looking up, with the new baby and all – he was really looking forward to it. He just seemed happy."

"And what about his dad, Jack?"

"Well, that's a very different story. He drank, and I mean a lot. Hadn't been out on the boat these last few years. His death is less surprising."

"And the other owner?"

Derek looked surprised.

"I just thought it was owned by Si and his old man. Never knew anyone else was involved."

"They may not be anymore, but I've been told that the RoseMarie was named after the wives of the two original owners. Do you know who they were?"

"That's not unusual, to name a boat after the wife… helps keep them quiet, I suppose." He smiled to take the sting out of his words. "Presumably, one of them would have been Jack's old lady but I don't know if she was the Rose or the Marie bit. The boats been around for years, so it would've been well before my time." He stood up. "Got to get back to cleaning up. Was there anything else?"

"No, you've been a great help, thank you."

He turned to go, but turned back.

"If you want stories about the old days and how Si's old man or anyone else got started, you want to talk to my dad George. You'll find him in The London Trader, five o'clock on the dot every day. He'll talk to anyone for a pint, or for nothing sometimes. In fact, it's hard to get him to stop."

Derek left.

"Are you going to eat those?" Kate asked, eyeing up Callie's remaining chips.

Callie pushed her plate towards Kate.

"He wasn't a great deal of help," Callie said, watching Kate add salt and vinegar to the chips.

"No, but it's not hard to guess where you'll be at five o'clock on the dot," Kate said between mouthfuls.

"Care to join me?"

"Can't. Some of us have to work for a living, I'll have you know."

As a solicitor specialising in criminal defence work, Kate spent most of her time defending drink or drug drivers and shoplifters on legal aid. Occasionally, her days were enlivened by a touch of fraud and even murder, but petty crime remained the core of her business. "But, if you're lucky," she added, "I might come along and find you at six if you are still there. And if George is as big a talker as his son was suggesting, you might well be."

Callie rather thought that might indeed be the case. She had high hopes of George.

Chapter 13

The London Trader was not a pub Callie usually frequented. Situated on the sea front, it often seemed to have groups of bikers or football fans gathered outside, but at five o'clock on a wet weekday off season there was a solitary smoker seated on the damp benches by the door and it didn't look much busier inside. Callie shook her umbrella out, pushed the door open and looked around. There were three people in the bar, all men, all elderly and all sitting separately, nursing their pints. As she entered, they all looked up with interest.

Callie smiled in their general directions and went up to the bar.

"Lime and soda, please," she asked the bartender, a man in his forties who looked as if he could hold his own in a ruck. Callie took another look around the pub as she waited for her drink. A television in the corner was tuned to a twenty-four-hour news channel, with a muted newsreader and a banner running along the bottom of the screen showing the headlines. Tearing her eyes away from the sadly predictable news that the FTSE was down, Callie saw a pool table at one end of the room and a dartboard at the other, with a previous game's scores still on the chalkboard.

"There you are," the barman said as he placed a startlingly green drink in front of her. It had ice and a swizzle stick in it, and the better part of a bottle of lime cordial, she concluded.

"Thank you." She tapped her card on the reader he held out. "Er, can you tell me if George is in?"

The barman nodded towards a bench between the jukebox and the fruit machine by way of answer. The elderly man sitting there looked up hopefully as Callie made her way over to him.

"Hello," she said, "are you Derek's dad?"

"For my sins," he replied. "What's he been telling you? If he said I owe him money, he's lying." He grinned to take any sting out of his words.

"Derek said you would be here and that you might be willing to talk to me."

"I always enjoy talking to pretty ladies," he said, with a laugh that revealed the few teeth he had left not looking too healthy. "Does my reputation the world of good." He looked round and raised his glass at the other old men, who were all looking a bit disgruntled that he had been the one she'd chosen.

Callie pulled up a stool and put her drink on the old and battered table.

"Derek said you might be willing to talk to me about the old days of fishing in Hastings," she said.

"Not much I don't know about fishing from here. It were a hard life back when I were a young 'un, not like now with their motorised winches and satellite navigation systems." And he was off down memory lane.

Callie couldn't get a word in edgeways for nearly fifteen minutes. She learnt more about how fishing used to be than she strictly needed to; it was all very interesting, but she felt sure that some of his stories were apocryphal, no matter how much he insisted he had seen it 'with me own eyes'.

Finally, George finished his beer with a smack of his lips and put his empty glass down. Callie had barely started on her own fluorescent drink.

"Thirsty work, this talking," he said.

Callie took the hint. However, when she brought his pint back, she made sure to get the first word in, in an attempt to steer the conversation back to where she wanted it.

"Did you know the original owners of the RoseMarie?"

"Jack Porter and Harry Hudson? Course I knew 'em. Both dead now. Sad business."

"Harry is dead too?"

"Yeah, cancer took him, oh, a couple of years back it must be, maybe more." He chuckled at a memory. "Harry was a character. Larger than life, he were. Used to call him 'Dirty Harry' back in the day on account of him shagging anything in a skirt."

"But he named the boat after his wife, along with Jack's wife, I was told."

"Of course he did, he knew how to keep his old lady sweet, and he couldn't really name the boat after all his girlfriends, could he? That would have been much too long a name." He laughed again, giving Callie an even better view of his rotten teeth.

"Did he have any children?"

"Not with Rose, he didn't. Couldn't say about his other women."

"And what happened to Rose?"

"Still lives here, somewhere, see her about. Face like a slapped arse; don't know what Harry ever saw in her. Definitely not his usual sort of girl. Came from money, mind." He laughed. "I suppose it was like in that TV show. You know the one, 'What first attracted you to the millionaire Paul Daniels?' What a question that was."

He laughed even harder and Callie saw to her dismay that he had almost finished his drink again, but he showed no signs of being drunk, so she fetched him another pint and hoped she wouldn't be responsible for him falling over on his way home.

"So, when Harry died, Jack Porter inherited sole ownership of the boat?" she asked. "Or does Harry's wife own half?"

George sipped his beer thoughtfully.

"Nah, now you come to mention it. I heard it was a bit odd. Harry left his share to Jack, I think."

"Why would he do that?"

"His wife weren't going to be going out on the boat, was she? I know there are some women doing it these days but it ain't right." He shook his head at the thought. "Unnatural, that's what it is."

Callie ignored this.

"So he left it to Jack?"

George shrugged.

"Don't rightly know but it didn't do him much good, that I do know."

"In what way?" Callie asked and George gave it some thought, and took a few more sips of beer, before answering.

"Well, Si and Jack had lots of rows after that, Si moved out the home, well, he had the missus by then so that was normal, but… Then there was the business with Surly Dick."

"Who?"

"Surly Dick. He lost his arm in an accident on the boat, blamed Jack and Simon."

"Oh, would that be Richard Simmons?"

"Aye, that's right. Jack stopped going out on the boat, pretty much handed it over to Si. Without work, Jack's drinking got out of hand and his old lady, Marie, she upped and left. Can't say as I blame her, really. Living with an angry man, like Jack was then, it can't have been easy."

There was a stir in the bar as the door opened and Kate bounced in.

"Hiya!" she called to Callie. "Can I get anyone a drink?"

"Mine's a pint of IPA, darlin'," George called out as he quickly finished the one he was drinking. "Friend of yours?" he asked Callie. "This is turning into a bit of a party! I'll just go and have a tinkle." He stood up unsteadily and made his way to the toilets.

"Who's your friend?" Kate asked as she came over, clutching two pints of beer and a glass of wine for Callie. "Derek's dad?"

"Yes." Callie looked dubiously at the white wine; it seemed rather too deep a yellow for a pinot.

"Yes, sorry, no pinot grigio, just what he said was a Sauvignon but I think I read Chardonnay on the bottle as he put it back."

Callie took a sip and grimaced.

"Yup, that's a Chardonnay," she said and looked between her two choices. A much too strong lime and soda or her least favourite wine, a Chardonnay. In the end, she fished what was left of the ice out of the soda and put it in the wine to dilute the oaky taste.

"Has he managed to tell you anything?" Kate asked.

"Yes, but I'm not sure of its significance," Callie told her as George came out of the gents, not quite done up, and re-joined them.

"I like a woman who drinks pints." George nodded at Kate's drink as he picked his own up and drank some.

"So, there was a falling out between Simon and Jack when Harry died, is that right?"

"There was a falling out between Jack and the whole world when that happened. Never got over it, he didn't."

"It seems a bit of an extreme reaction," Kate said, and Callie had to agree.

"And Jack's wife, Marie, she still lives in Hastings, doesn't she?"

"That's right. Stayed close to keep an eye on the boys, I reckon, even if they didn't want to see her... well, Si didn't. He wouldn't have nothing to do with her after she left, but Carl's still her little boy, and she's all he's got left now." He shook his head at the thought.

It quickly became clear that George had little left that he could tell them about the Hudsons and the Porters, although he had a lot of other stories, some of which Callie had already heard. So Callie and Kate left George to his thoughts, and her wine pretty much untouched on the table in front of him.

"He can certainly put them away," Kate commented as they walked up the High Street. "Let's cut through Courthouse Street and go to The Crown." She turned down the side street as she talked. "How many pints did you buy him, anyway?"

"Too many," Callie replied.

They pushed through the smokers that always hung around outside every pub in town, no matter how cold and wet the weather, and went into the warm.

"Mmm, I love this place," Kate said, breathing in the delicious aromas of Irish stew and saag aloo curry.

They found a table in the corner and sat down.

"I'll get the drinks in and grab a menu." Kate hurried to the bar, giving Callie time to mentally sort through everything she had learnt from Old George. Discarding the apocryphal fisherman stories, she was left with the strange account of the breakdown of the Porter family. Kate was back quite quickly with, Callie was relieved to see, a better-looking glass of wine, with one ice cube already in it.

"So, what else did George have to say?" Kate asked, half her attention on the menu she had brought back. "Anything useful?"

"I don't honestly know," Callie told her. "Harry Hudson, one of the original two owners of the RoseMarie, left his share of the boat to Simon when he died. Not his wife Rose nor his business partner Jack. Now why would he do that?"

"Maybe he didn't like his wife or his partner."

"Good point – and his wife came from money, so maybe he thought she didn't need it."

"Makes sense. And maybe Jack's drinking was already getting out of hand and he didn't want him pissing it up the wall. Old George said Simon was a natural at the job."

"Very true," Callie said. She could see the sense in that. "Yes, that would explain it perfectly, and I can also see why that caused the ructions it apparently did. Jack could have resented the fact that his son was now his equal, and Carl would resent them both because he hadn't been given anything."

Marie Porter would know, Callie thought. Perhaps she could hang around her address and try and engineer a chat because, for the life of her, she couldn't think of a legitimate reason for her to visit.

"Old Harry should have left his share to be divided between the two boys. That would have been fairer, even if the younger one was hopeless," Kate said, then went back to looking at the menu. "Now, what are you going to have to eat? Are we having starters? Just a main? Or going straight in for a pudding or two? Apple fritters and hot cross bun ice-cream?"

* * *

I've watched her over the years. The good time girl, the mother, the adulteress, the deserter, the lush. Hanging around bars picking up men, even though she's no spring chicken, no one's first choice. She is often left sitting on her own at closing time, drowning her sorrows with a glass of pink gin.

And tonight is the same. Just as the others have done, she makes it easy for me. She gets off the bar stool, lipstick leaking into the wrinkles around her mouth, mascara smeared under her baggy, bleary eyes. It's not hard to follow her home, stumbling, drunk, completely unaware of how much danger she is in.

When she gets to the tatty old house converted into flats that she calls home, has called home since she ran out on her family, she stands at the top of the steps down to the basement and fumbles in her bag for her keys. She hasn't noticed me and is taken by surprise when I push her. She goes head first down the steps and lands by her front door. I would have liked for her to have broken her neck in the fall, but unfortunately, she hasn't. That would have been too easy.

She tries to sit up, confused by what has happened and I hurry down the steps. Her keys have fallen out of her bag and are on the ground next to her. I grab them.

"Wha–" is all she can say before I have opened the door and pulled her inside. She is sprawling on the floor. "Wha' are you doing here? What's going on?" she slurs and tries to get up, so I kick her legs out from under her, grab her hair and pull her into the living room. She struggles, kicking and biting, surprising me. She's strong for such an old bird, but a swift punch to her face and she is down again, out for the count. I take my chance and grip her round the neck, pressing hard. She comes round a little and tries instinctively to stop me, moving her head, clawing at my hands. But she is weaker than me now, drunk and disorientated by the punch to her head, and not a match for my anger.

It is over quickly.

I feel elated. It's the first time I have actually killed someone with my own hands and I am surprised at how good it feels, even through the double gloves I have put on to be sure not to leave any prints. Much better than snapping a fish's neck or dropping a crab into boiling water. This is real killing. And I find it exciting.

Now I have to clean up, make sure I remove any trace of me. But first, I want to dress the scene. I have to complete the picture I have in my head, that I have had in my head all this time. I reach for the rope in my bag.

Chapter 14

Callie was busy with a telephone clinic the next morning when she got a call from the duty sergeant.

"Sudden death reported, Sea View Villa," he told her and gave her the details. She hurriedly called Linda, the practice manager, to explain what had happened and to apologise. She promised that she would work longer that afternoon to make sure everyone on her list was contacted that day, but meanwhile, she asked Linda to see if one of her colleagues had a free moment, despite knowing this was unlikely. If so – she asked with her fingers crossed – could they deal with some of the list for her?

These call-outs were a regular occurrence, and her colleagues resented the fact that she so often left them with extra work. At the same time, they all knew she was only part-time and therefore paid less, and she regularly put in more than her paid hours. This made her feel less guilty even if it didn't make her colleagues any happier.

The name Sea View Villa could have been challenged under the Trade Descriptions Act, attached as it was to a rather tired-looking conversion of a semi-detached Victorian that could only possibly have a view of the sea from the top of the roof. There were six flats if the number of doorbells were anything to go by. The police officer, sheltering from the rain in his car parked in the street outside, directed her down a short flight of stairs to a small, covered area by the door to the basement. A second police officer was waiting for her there, keeping out of the rain as best he could.

"Room at the back," he told her. "Woman, hanged."

Callie nodded and felt the hairs on the back of her neck stand up. Another hanging? This had to be more than a coincidence. She put down her bag and took out her crime-scene coveralls. As she bent down to pull them over her feet, she spotted a smear of blood on the bottom step and another on the wall.

"Sorry, but you are going to have to move to the top of the stairs," she told the police officer, pointing to the stains. "Just until I am certain this isn't a crime scene."

With a sigh, he did as he was told and Callie quickly pulled on the rest of her protective clothing and opened the front door, marked as Flat 1, with her gloved hand.

Standing just inside the door, she started looking around. She was in a dark, narrow hallway, with the only light coming from the open door to the kitchen and, at the far end, a partially open door that led to what looked to be a sitting room. The doormat was halfway down the dim corridor, rucked up and tilted sideways as if it had been pulled along. Carefully placing her feet on either side of the narrow walkway so as not to disturb any footprints that might or might not be there, she made her way towards the back of the flat, passing the open door to the kitchen. A brief look inside showed a tidy space and nothing untoward. There were two further doors, both closed. One had a rather kitsch, ceramic depiction of a child sitting on a toilet painted on it, which probably meant it led to the bathroom. The other door presumably led to a bedroom.

Reaching the end of the hallway, Callie pushed the half-open door with her hand and met some resistance. Slipping through the gap, she turned and saw that the resistance was caused by the body hanging from the back of it. Stepping away from the grotesque, doll-like body, Callie took time to assess the situation.

The woman had a rope around her neck, very similar to the ropes that had been found at the two previous scenes. It was attached to the door by an over-door hook. She had seen similar ones advertised for bedrooms and bathrooms; they were meant for hanging dressing gowns or towels, not people, but this seemed to be one designed to support greater weight. Even so, she was surprised it was sturdy enough to hold a fully-grown adult.

The woman's legs were splayed and dragging on the floor. She would have been able to stand and relieve the pressure on her neck if she had wanted to – if she hadn't already been dead when she was strung up, which Callie was pretty sure she had been. Aside from the bruising to her face and the dried blood that had come from her nose, a split lip and a cut somewhere in her hairline, Callie could see livid finger marks on the woman's neck, either side of the rope. Like Jack Porter, this woman's hanging was just window-dressing. The question was why.

The face seemed vaguely familiar, but it was hard to tell with the injuries; Callie couldn't remember where she had seen this woman before. Perhaps she was a patient, although the surgery in Ore would be closer to where she lived.

Once Callie had finished her cursory examination, she backed out of the room, retracing her route out of the flat as best as she could.

Wishing she had thought to bring an umbrella, Callie hurried up the steps. Pulling off her gloves, she approached the police car where both of the officers were now keeping watch.

"Definite suspicious death, we'll need the full forensic team and you'll need to let DI Miller know," she told them.

The older of the two immediately reached for his radio.

"Who found the body?" she asked the other officer.

"The son. I sent him home but I've got the details." He pulled his notebook out. "Carl Porter. His mum wasn't answering her phone so he came to check on her." He stopped as Callie let out a low moan. Flat 1, 12, Marshalls Road, was the address she had copied from Miller's files. His records hadn't named the house as Sea View Villa, that's why she hadn't recognised Marie Porter's address straight away.

* * *

Callie was sheltering in her car when a silver Mondeo pulled up a little way down the street. Thankful that the rain had finally stopped, Callie stepped out to meet Miller and Jeffries as they walked towards the scene. Colin Brewer, the short and square crime scene manager was busy setting a perimeter which stopped them from getting close to the flat entrance.

"Another hanging?" Miller queried as he reached Callie.

"After she'd been beaten up and manually strangled, yes."

"Oh." Miller gave her a questioning look but the way she stared back at him put him off asking her if she was sure. Instead, he turned his attention to the forensic team, who were busy unloading equipment from a van.

"Not to mention that this is another member of the same family," she added.

Both Miller and Jeffries looked up in interest at that bit of news.

"Not the other son?" Miller asked.

"No, the mother, Marie," Callie told him. "Although Carl found the body."

"Is he here?" Jeffries asked.

"They let him go home," Callie answered with a shake of her head. "Although isn't his home still a crime scene? If so, I'm not sure where he is staying. The officers who let him go have his details." She checked her watch. "I've got to leave, get back to work." She looked at Miller. "I'll catch up later?"

"Yes, but it might be quite late," said Miller.

He had a concerned expression on his face and Callie sensed he would be worrying about his earlier decision not to go all-out on the first two deaths. She just hoped he had at least kept the scenes intact and not let Carl move back home, because any evidence would have long since been lost if he had.

* * *

"This killer is annihilating the family," Callie said to Miller much later, when he finally arrived at her place, carrying a bottle of wine and an Indian takeaway.

"That's only true if they are all murders."

"You can't seriously think that Marie Porter strangled herself."

"No." He hesitated, unsure of how exactly to put his thoughts across. "But what if Simon killed himself because of some problem in his relationship with his dad and his involvement with drugs, the business going tits up, or because he thinks the world's against him or something, and then the father dies of a drug-and-drink overdose? Carl blames the dad, and when he finds his body, strings him up as a way of showing he was to blame for Si's death. That works, doesn't it?"

Callie had to admit it did.

"But what about Marie? Doesn't that change everything?"

"Possibly, unless she was the root cause of the family break-up and he blames her for it."

"So what? You think Carl suddenly escalates from mock hanging his dad to killing his mum?"

"He stands to gain the most, and he's been the one to find the body every time. He has to be a suspect."

"You aren't seriously suggesting he killed them all, are you? I really can't believe that. They are his family, for goodness' sake."

"There are lots of cases where that happens, and I have to consider him for it, at least until he gives some kind of alibi. After all, he's the only one to benefit. He is now sole owner of the RoseMarie and it must be worth a bit."

"What about Simon's wife? Wouldn't she inherit his half?"

Miller stopped mid-chew.

"Possibly, but I can't really see a heavily pregnant woman being able to do all this, can you?" he said.

Callie could see his point, but equally Carl finding all three members of his family and making himself the main suspect still seemed like a pretty stupid way to go about things.

"Have you spoken to him?" she asked.

"Not yet, we, um, aren't sure where he is right now."

Callie could see that changed things. She remembered the police officer at the crime scene telling her he had Carl's details.

"He didn't give the officer the right address?"

"No, well, yes. He gave his home one, where he lived with his dad, but he isn't staying there."

"Can't say that I blame him." Callie wouldn't want to go back there if she was him, either. "And you don't have another address for him? From before?"

"He had told us when we moved him out that he would be staying with his mum, but he wasn't."

Callie thought about it.

"He's probably just staying with a friend. At least I hope he is, I mean, that poor lad, he's lost his whole family," she said.

Miller didn't look convinced.

"Did you check Carl's alibis for the first two deaths?" she asked.

"First thing I did when we realised he wasn't where he said he would be, and they're not exactly cast iron. When his brother died, he was out drinking with mates, then walked home and, of course, his dad was too drunk to confirm what time he got in, or even if he got in at all. And it's similar for Jack's death — out drinking again. The only time we can confirm with any certainty is when he made the call to emergency services in both cases. Obviously, we'll be going back over the two nights and interviewing all his friends and the pubs he said he was in, checking CCTV, the works."

Callie said nothing. It would be difficult to confirm with any degree of certainty now that more than a week had gone by since the first death. People, especially heavy drinkers, forget and get muddled about which night was which. Could they be sure when he was with them and when he left? She didn't think many of his friends would be able to recall that, if any. With luck, there might be CCTV somewhere to confirm it. Thankfully most places stored images on the cloud and there wasn't the old problem of tapes being wiped and reused, but it would take time to collect and check it all. There was no doubt in her mind that the delay in treating the first two deaths as murder would make any investigation now that much harder. But one look at Miller showed her that he didn't need her to tell him that.

"Are you going to do a public appeal? See if anyone comes forward and says they saw him?"

Miller sighed. She knew he hated public speaking of any kind.

"Press conference at nine," he said. "And we're trying to play down any idea that the three deaths are all murders."

"But they are."

"We don't know that and we don't want the general public getting their knickers in a twist and panicking."

"Then all you have to say is that all three deaths are connected and outsiders are not at risk."

"You know what the headlines will be if we do: 'Serial killer at large in Hastings', and no one will read any further than that. We discussed it at a senior team meeting and decided that we have to present the first two deaths as a suicide and an accidental overdose."

Callie knew that he probably didn't really have much choice in the matter, but it still irritated her that he wasn't taking the first two deaths seriously, or at least, not seriously enough.

Miller could see she wasn't happy. He looked at his watch.

"I'd better get home," he said. "Get a good night's sleep. Don't want to look old and tired for the cameras." He got up and, with a quick peck on her cheek, left Callie to do the clearing up. As usual.

Chapter 15

The next day, Linda caught a glimpse of Callie walking quickly through the office on the way to the kitchen, and said, "Can you please do something about Mr Herring?"

Callie thought she should know better than to try and slip through unnoticed; it never worked. "What's he done now?" she asked.

"Apart from ringing five times already this morning?"

"Five? That's a lot even for him."

"And we have better things to do than act as his personal messenger, so call him back." Linda turned back to her computer, then added, "Please."

"Will do," Callie hastily reassured the office manager, but still headed for the kitchen. Not even an emergency with Mr Herring was going to come between her and her morning coffee. She needed one after watching a recording of the morning press conference. Miller, looking well-rested and smart in a crisp white shirt and dark tie, had done exactly as he said he would the night before. His statement left the distinct impression that the first two deaths were tragic but not suspicious, although he had revealed that Marie Porter was murdered. He had then launched straight into an appeal for Carl Porter to come forward and help with their enquiries into his mother's death. Everyone would have been left in no doubt whatsoever that Carl was the main, indeed only, suspect in his mother's murder inquiry. Callie was furious.

* * *

It was well into the afternoon before Callie managed to get to visit Mr Herring. She was still angry about the press conference and was ready to do battle with her difficult and demanding patient. Once again, he had insisted he was unable to come to the surgery due to his high levels of anxiety, but at least he hadn't asked her to bring milk this time.

When she arrived and knocked on his door, they went through the rigmarole of him confirming her identity before he would open up the bolts and locks. When she finally got to look at him, if anything, he seemed even more anxious than before. His hair was standing on end, he had several days' worth of stubble on his face and had visibly lost weight since the last time she had seen him. In short, he looked unkempt and a little unhinged.

"Come in, Dr Hughes, come in," he whispered and quickly stood to one side to allow her to get past him. He then carefully closed, locked and bolted the door, and ushered her into the kitchen before speaking, or rather whispering, again.

"This can't go on, Mr Herring," she began firmly but he wasn't listening.

"I can't go on like this, Doctor. You've got to help me. They're going to kill me – I heard them talking about it!"

"About killing you?"

"Yes! They said they'd slit my throat. I heard them, they were laughing when they said it, but they meant it, I know they did."

Callie sighed. Mr Herring had never shown that he had a sense of humour or that he knew when people were just trying to wind him up, so she perfectly understood that he would take a jokey comment, particularly one in such bad taste, at face value.

"I'm sure they didn't really mean it." She tried to reassure him, but he was having none of it.

"No, no, they did. I know they did, and they've made other threats too and the man, he pushed me and jabbed me with his finger when he told me not to complain about them again. He bruised me. Look." He undid his shirt and showed Callie a small round bruise on his chest wall.

She had to admit, that did sound as if the man, at least, had acted in a threatening way and committed a minor assault. She also had to acknowledge that Mr Herring could be very irritating.

"Have you been to the police, told them about the threat to you?"

"Yes, of course, and they just made it worse. They came around, spoke to the woman next door and she said they'd just been joking, but they weren't. I know they weren't." He was wringing his hands as he spoke and was clearly terrified.

Callie was having difficulty making sense of what he was saying.

"They talked to the old lady next door? Mrs Caldwell?" she asked.

"No, no, the young woman who is supposed to be looking after her. Fine carer she is, drinking and playing loud music all day – well, when she's there, anyway. She goes off with her friends and leaves poor Mrs Caldwell alone for hours." He leant closer so that he could speak even more quietly. "I hear her crying sometimes, calling for help."

"Who? The carer?"

"No! Mrs Caldwell. When they leave her alone, I hear her then."

"Have you been round to see if you could help?"

"No!" He seemed alarmed at the thought. "I mentioned it, said I could come and sit with her if it would help. That's when they threatened me."

When Callie thought back to how Mrs Caldwell had been happy to help Mr Herring when he was unwell, it was the least he could do to help her now that it sounded as if she needed the support. It seemed strange that her carers weren't keen to accept the offer.

"Are they there now?"

He grabbed her arm.

"Please don't go round there – they'll blame me."

"But what do you want me to do, then?"

The doorbell rang at that moment and he froze, terrified. Then, it rang again.

"Aren't you going to answer it?" she asked.

"I'm not expecting anyone," he said and gave a frightened gasp as a man appeared at the kitchen window and gave them a little wave.

"Mr Herring?" The middle-aged man, smartly dressed in a dark grey suit and a black tie, didn't look in the least bit threatening to Callie. "I'm from Phillips, here for our appointment." The man spoke loudly and clearly so that they could hear him through the window.

Phillips were a firm of local undertakers, Callie had worked with them on many occasions. She recognised the man as one of their staff, so she smiled and moved towards the door.

"No! I didn't ask you to come!" Mr Herring shouted back to him. "Go away! Go away!"

Callie looked at her patient in surprise, as did the man outside. Freddy or Frank, she couldn't remember the name, looked puzzled, checked the details on his phone and held it up.

"Look," he said. "Here. 2 pm. A Mr Herring, at this address, with regard to his mother."

Callie leant across the sink and looked closely at the screen, it did indeed say Mr Herring and gave the correct address.

"But I didn't make the appointment!" Mr Herring said, almost hysterical. "I don't want to speak to you!" Then, he darted out of the kitchen, across the hall and into the back bedroom, closing the door behind him.

Callie sighed and tried to open the window. Needless to say, it was locked and the key wasn't anywhere to be seen. Goodness only knew how Mr Herring would get out if there was a fire, or how anyone would be able to get in if he was actually taken ill.

Indicating that she was going to the door, Callie went into the hallway and began the laborious process of unlocking it. Fortunately, Mr Herring had left the key in the deadlock, so she was able to open up.

"Oh, hello, Dr Hughes," Frank or Freddy said, smiling. "Are you the deceased's doctor?"

"No, there isn't a deceased – as far as I know, anyway. His mother died a couple of years ago and has already been buried. Mr Herring says he hasn't made the appointment with you, so there must be some mistake." Which didn't explain why they had his name and address, though.

Freddy, or Frank, was looking very confused, which was understandable. "Oh, I'm very sorry about that," he said. "I can't imagine what can have happened."

"I suspect someone must be playing a prank on him or something like that."

"Oh dear, that's not very nice, not very nice at all, for him, or for us. I mean, it's a wasted journey. Please, apologise to Mr Herring and explain that we are as much victims of this as he is."

"Of course, and I'm very sorry you've been troubled."

"Not at all, Dr Hughes. I'll mark any future appointments for Mr Herring to be confirmed in writing or in person before being accepted. I've noted his details."

Frank or Freddy turned and went on his way.

Callie locked up, and leant against the door. It appeared that it wasn't all in her patient's mind, his neighbours really were waging a campaign against him. She rubbed her forehead, aware that a headache was just beginning. What with her anger at Miller and now this, she needed to calm down or release the tension in some way. She took a few deep breaths and then went to Mr Herring's back bedroom door and knocked on it.

"Can I come in, Mr Herring?"

"Has he gone?"

"Yes, and he apologised for upsetting you, although, I can't see that it was his fault."

The door slowly opened and Mr Herring peered out. It looked as if he had been crying.

"I didn't make the appointment, I'm sure I didn't or any appointment with any of the people who have been turning up insisting that I have," he said as he let her in and sat on the small single bed under the window. Callie came into the room and looked around. It had been Mr Herring's room when he was caring for his mother, but after her death he had moved into the main bedroom. This, along with the sitting room, had an adjoining wall with Mrs Caldwell's flat and therefore was no longer an option for him due to the noise – although all was quiet at the moment. Callie went and sat on the small chair by the dressing table.

"I know you didn't," she said. "So that begs the question, who did?"

Mr Herring just shrugged. He was wringing his hands and staring at the floor.

"You said this has happened before?"

"Not undertakers, but other things."

"Like what?"

"A man came round saying I wanted him to write my will, and there was a pest control company saying I'd told them I had bed bugs." His hands flopped onto his lap in despair. "I don't remember making any of these appointments. Why would I? No one has died, I already have a will, and I don't have bed bugs. Why would I ask these people to call?"

"You really don't remember making the appointments?"

"No! But do you think I am… I keep wondering if it is really me doing this, and I just can't remember. Do you think I'm going mad?"

"No, I don't. I think someone is playing some seriously unfunny jokes on you." Callie glanced in the direction of Mrs Caldwell's flat.

Mr Herring closed his eyes and shuddered.

"There's nothing I can do about it, is there?" he asked her.

"You can ask them to stop," she said. But one look at his face told her that he wasn't going to do that. "You can report them to the council for harassment, but it's a hard one to prove."

"And it would just make things worse."

"Or you can wait it out. They will get bored pretty soon if you don't react."

At least she hoped they would.

When she finally left Mr Herring, hearing him lock himself securely in his home again, Callie paused outside the door of Mrs Caldwell's flat next door. There was no sound coming from it. No music, and no crying or pleas for help, either. Looking round and making sure that she couldn't hear anyone coming up the stairs to the walkway, Callie knocked on the door. There was no response, so she knocked again.

"Hello? Mrs Caldwell? It's Dr Hughes from the surgery. I'm just calling round to see if you are okay."

She listened intently but there was no response. Absolutely nothing that she could hear at all. She wasn't sure what she should do, but this time, she knew she had to do something.

Chapter 16

Callie called into the police station on her way back from Mr Herring's flat. She wanted to speak to Miller and tell him that she thought he was wrong to put out the idea that Carl was a suspect in, at the least, the murder of his mother, but he wasn't there.

"There was a report of Carl being seen in St Leonard's," Detective Sergeant Jayne Hales explained. "He and Bob Jeffries have gone to check it out."

Callie had known Jayne from when the detective had still been a uniformed constable with a knack of being able to deal with stroppy prostitutes without upsetting them further. She had helped Callie on many occasions and they had become friends as well as colleagues.

"Is it just me who doesn't think Carl killed his mother?" Callie asked her.

"Whether he did or didn't, he has questions to answer." Jayne wasn't going to openly disagree with her boss. "So he needs to come in."

Callie supposed she was right.

"What a day," Callie said.

"Do you want a cuppa?"

"No, no, you're all right, Jayne, I need to try and catch a social worker before she knocks off for the day." Callie looked at her watch. "If she hasn't already done so."

Callie hurried out, down the hill and away from the modern police station to the rather older and more dilapidated building that housed the social work department, where she popped her head around the door of the messiest office she had ever seen; well, at least since the last time she had been in Helen Austen's office, anyway. The social worker seemed to know where everything was amongst the files and pieces of paper that were scattered over the desk and computer keyboard, but Callie never understood how she did. A bump in the bits of paper indicated where the computer mouse was probably hidden, and a telephone was on the windowsill with the receiver off the hook, which probably explained why Callie hadn't been able to get through to her when she tried. How anyone ever managed to work in this chaos was a mystery.

"Hi, Helen," Callie said and entered the room.

"Callie! To what do I owe this pleasure?" Helen said with a wide smile as she moved a stack of files from a chair and gestured for Callie to sit down. Helen was smartly dressed in brighter colours than Callie ever had the nerve to wear, and had a pair of reading glasses perched on her head. This seemed a sensible precaution, because if she put them down anywhere on the desk, she would never find them again.

"Can I talk to you about one of my patients that I'm a bit worried about?"

"You can talk to me any time, so long as you don't expect me to magic up twenty-four-hour care or a place in a supported living centre."

"No, I just want to pick your brains, if you don't mind."

"Not at all, pick away, in fact, it's a relief that you don't want anything more than that."

"Well, not yet, anyway," Callie admitted. "It's an old lady, a patient at my surgery, who until recently lived on her own but now seems to have two young people living there, looking after her."

"Lucky woman."

"Yes, well, possibly. Would the carers have been organised through your department?"

"Good heavens, no! Two carers living with the client? Has to be a private arrangement. We just don't have the manpower or the money to provide that level of care in the home."

"Well, that makes it easier in some ways, but not in others."

"Do you have concerns about the standard of care they are giving?"

"Yes. Apparently sometimes the lady, my patient, can be heard crying and calling for help." Callie held her hand up as Helen looked ready to speak. "I'm well aware that sometimes people with dementia and such like can be confused and might call for help when they are being perfectly well-cared for, but I have to admit I'm worried."

"Have you been in to see how she is? Does she look well cared for?"

"I haven't been able to − that's one of my concerns. I've called to try and set up a visit, but the home number has been disconnected and we don't have any records of other numbers or next-of-kin details. I even called round when I was in the area but no one answered the door."

"Hm, that is worrying. You don't have a record of who is providing the care?"

"No, we have no details whatsoever."

Helen started shuffling through some of the bits of paper on the top of the filing cabinet, presumably waiting to be filed.

"Now somewhere here…" Helen pulled a piece of paper from the pile, goodness only knew how she managed to pick the right one, as it had nothing on it to make it stand out from the rest. "List of registered care providers, I knew I'd seen it recently." She handed it to Callie. "But if she or a family member have organised something between themselves, they may not even be registered."

"That's what I'm afraid of, but this is at least a place to start." Callie looked at the list. There seemed an awful lot of them and mostly they were names she recognised as they provided care for social services as well as privately.

"What do I do if it isn't one of these, and I have concerns about the standard of care being provided?"

"Get back to me, but you must realise the legal position is difficult. We can't just march in there and demand to see the woman. It's her home. Someone has to make a formal complaint of neglect or abuse. Are there any family members you can talk to?"

"Not that I know of; it was the first thing I checked. We have none on record and I've spoken to all my colleagues, but no one has been to see her in ages. She's had no contact with us, not even repeat prescriptions, and she's always been healthy until – well, according to her neighbour it sounds like she developed dementia."

"Then how did she make arrangements for care? Someone must have done that and someone must be paying them. I bet there are relatives lurking in the background somewhere; you've just got to play at detective and find out who they are."

There was a knock and Helen's assistant poked her head around the door.

"You've left your phone off the hook again, Helen, and Mr Townsend wants to talk to you."

"Only way I get any peace and quiet," Helen whispered to Callie as she obediently put the receiver back in place.

"I'll put him through then," the assistant said and left.

"I'll leave you to it, Helen. Thanks for your help," Callie said as the phone started ringing and Helen waved goodbye as she reached for it.

* * *

"Hello, this is Dr Hughes from the Old Town Surgery. I'm calling to find about private care providers and I'm particularly interested in finding out who is providing care for a patient of mine, a Mrs Elizabeth Caldwell, known as Betty." Callie was on the final name on Helen's list. So far, no one had admitted to organising care for Mrs Caldwell, so it was looking increasingly likely that this was a private arrangement entered into by members of Mrs Caldwell's family. The problem was that she couldn't find any record of a family that she could ask. That didn't mean there wasn't anyone, just that they weren't patients at her practice and that Mrs Caldwell had never felt the need to update them on who her next of kin was after her husband had died.

"I'm pretty sure we don't have anyone on the books by that name," the care provider answered her. "Let me just check for you… no, not one of ours, I'm afraid. Can I help you with anything else, Dr Hughes?"

Callie put down her phone and wondered exactly what she should do next, but having drawn a blank so far, her only real option was to visit Mrs Caldwell, and keep visiting until she found the carers in. Then she would have to insist on seeing her patient to reassure herself that she was being well cared for. This was all thanks to Mr Herring. She rubbed at the spot between her eyes; she could feel a tension headache coming on.

* * *

Three down, two to go. Who's next? That's the question of the moment. They are all guilty, but some are more guilty than others. That doesn't mean I'm going to let any of them get away with it, though. No, not at all. I've dealt with the worst offenders, and not yet got caught, so now I can move onto the lesser ones, the lesser two. They weren't the ones who came up with the plan but they were instrumental in what happened, crucial in fact, and they have never attempted to put things right. They need to pay for that. Then I can rest. Then I will be at peace.

Chapter 17

Callie was in Porters wine bar having dinner with Steve Miller. It had long been a favourite haunt where she could relax with friends like Kate or Steve. The problem was, it had also been first choice as the place to go with Billy, so her feelings about it were now a little bit complicated.

Miller was, as usual, tucking into the steak pie, whilst Callie had opted for a Caesar salad with grilled chicken, but couldn't help looking enviously at the table next door where they had ordered the calorie-laden truffle mac and cheese.

"You didn't manage to find any relatives for this patient of yours?" he asked, breaking into her thoughts.

"No. I don't think she has any."

"Not much you can do, then, is there?"

"I'll keep trying," she replied, trying not to sound irritated by his lack of empathy. "I mean, someone must have organised the carers for her. Although it seems like it has to be a private arrangement because none of the registered care companies have her on their list."

"Hmm."

Callie didn't consider that an adequate response, so she looked at him and realised that he was too absorbed in his own thoughts, and the pie.

"What do you think?" she asked.

He just shrugged, his mind already elsewhere – he probably hadn't heard a word she had said.

She tapped his plate with her knife to get his attention. "Is everything all right?"

"Fine, fine, just work's a bit hectic." He checked his watch. "I'll need to get back when we're done here."

So much for a romantic dinner, Callie thought.

"Did you find Carl Porter?"

"Not yet, no. That's why I really have to go." He signalled to the waitress that he needed to pay.

"Don't worry, I'll get that," she told him. He might have finished eating but she was only halfway through her salad. "Will I see you later?" She wasn't sure he wanted to, given how uncommunicative he was being.

"Er, probably not, it's going to be a late one." He stood up and grabbed his coat.

He was probably helping stake out somewhere Carl might be staying, she thought. She didn't envy him the long night in a cold car, waiting for a sign his suspect was there. She'd helped out with a surveillance operation that needed a doctor's presence once and found it tedious and uncomfortable. She wouldn't be so keen to volunteer again.

Miller bent down and pecked her on the cheek awkwardly, knowing that she wasn't a fan of public shows of affection. "I'll see you tomorrow," he said and was gone.

Callie wasn't cross that he had left her in the lurch. In fact she was a little relieved, because it gave her an excuse to carry on with her plan to visit Mrs Caldwell at night when the carers must surely be in.

*　*　*

It was still quite early when she got to the block of flats where Mr Herring and Mrs Caldwell lived, but it was the first time she had visited the estate in the dark and now realised how few lights there were, and those that were on and working were so dim as to barely improve the situation. The rain was falling steadily, and her umbrella limited her view even more. Fortunately, she was able to locate Mrs Caldwell's flat quite easily, simply by following the sound of music. It wasn't anything she recognised as she was not a fan of heavy metal. No wonder it was driving Mr Herring crazy – or crazier, she thought. She had to wonder if any other residents had complained – she certainly would have if she had lived there.

Making her way gingerly along the balcony, trying not to trip over or step in anything nasty, Callie hesitated in front of Mrs Caldwell's door. Should she warn Mr Herring about her visit? Deciding against it, as it would only have sent him into a fit of anxiety, she knocked on the door and rang the bell. She couldn't hear over the cacophony emanating from the flat whether the bell had rung, and there was no response, so she tried again, banging louder this time. The door was pulled open by a young man dressed in a grubby tracksuit and with bare feet. Callie couldn't help but notice that his toenails needed cutting as she waved away the cannabis smoke that the open door had released.

"Fuck off and stop moaning," were the first words out of the young man's mouth, before he had really taken in who was standing there. Then he managed to focus better and added, "Who the fuck are you?"

"Erm, my name is Dr Hughes," Callie replied loudly. "I'm here to see Mrs Caldwell."

He looked confused for a moment and Callie was relieved when the ear-splitting music suddenly stopped.

"Who is it?" a female inside the flat called out.

"It's a doctor," the male answered, over his shoulder. "Wants to see the old lady."

The door was wrenched further open by a thin woman who looked to be in her thirties, but Callie, used to seeing how drugs, cigarettes and alcohol aged a person prematurely, knew she might well only be in her twenties.

The woman elbowed the lad out of the way and confronted Callie.

"She's asleep and I'm not going to wake her, not at this time of night," the woman said. "You'll have to come back, oh, and maybe make an appointment next time. It's only polite." She went to close the door, but Callie held firm, stopping her from doing so.

"I have already tried calling, but the phone number we have is no longer in use, and I have also called round before, and left a note, but there was no answer."

"Haven't seen a note, have you, Ty?" she asked the lad.

He shook his head.

"Can I ask who your employer is? One of the care agencies? A relative?" Callie persisted.

"Mrs Caldwell asked us to look after her and that's what we're doing. Looking out for her and stopping busybodies like you from disturbing her sleep."

Callie didn't say that the music that had been on earlier was likely to be much more of a disturbance.

"If I could just see her for a minute, then I'll be able to get out of your hair."

"No, it's not happening, so jog on and leave us be."

Callie stood her ground.

"I insist you let me in to see Mrs Caldwell for a welfare check or I will be forced to involve the police."

"And I'll be forced to make a complaint about you, disturbing law-abiding people in the middle of the night. Which surgery are you from? The one by the fishing sheds? I'll put in a formal complaint tomorrow."

The door closed before Callie could respond.

"Please do," she shouted through the closed door, just as the music was switched back on.

* * *

"What do you think I should do?" Callie asked Kate. She had phoned her friend as soon as she got back to her own flat, wet, angry and temporarily at a loss. "I'm pretty sure that Mrs Caldwell isn't being looked after properly. In fact, I don't even know if she's still alive." Callie had never had a case where she was unable to see a patient and ascertain whether or not they were receiving good care. She had many, many patients who didn't come in to the surgery because they didn't want her to tell them to stop doing something like smoking or drinking. There were a few who didn't want her help and who wouldn't let her into their homes because they didn't want her to see just how bad their accommodation was, because of dirt or hoarding, or they feared being put in a home against their wishes, but she had always been able to speak to the person themselves and make sure the decision was truly made by them and of their own free will. Until now.

"And you've been and seen your mate in social services?"

"Yes, she said it was dodgy legal ground as my patient wasn't a client of theirs and they couldn't just barge in there demanding to see her, unless I had some sort of proof that she was being ill-treated. I'll try her again now that I've been refused entry, but I suspect that even if I do get her to come along with me, we'll still be told exactly where to go."

"Then I don't think you have any choice but to involve the police. Ask them to accompany you and confirm that Mrs Caldwell is alive and well and, more to the point, happy with the level of care she is receiving."

"If she's capable of that. According to Mr Herring she was a bit confused before they even arrived on the scene, but yes, I know you are right. I'll get onto it first thing tomorrow."

"Why don't you just tell Steve now, or isn't he with you tonight?"

"No, he's not moved in, I'll have you know."

"Quite right, you don't want to rush into things, but you could at least call him and ask his advice, couldn't you?"

"Not really. He's out trying to find Carl, the poor boy whose family seem to be dying like flies, so it's probably not a good time. It can wait until the morning."

And maybe he wasn't the best person to ask, Callie thought to herself; she couldn't go running to him with every problem. Jayne Hales was probably a better choice in the circumstances.

"That poor lad. I think I'd also run away and hide if most of my family had been killed," said Kate.

"Quite, but the police regard that as suspicious behaviour, added to which he was the one to find all the corpses."

"Well, of course he was! They were all his nearest and dearest, weren't they? Honestly, what is Steve like?"

Callie hadn't actually mentioned that it was Miller who believed Carl to be a suspect, and she didn't rush in to try and defend him. She heartily agreed with Kate and couldn't really see Carl as anything other than a victim.

It was good that it was much later when he finally called to wish her good night and tell her the outcome of his evening's work.

"We got him!" Miller said immediately, unable to keep the triumphant tone from his voice.

"You found Carl? Thank goodness. Is he okay?"

"Of course." Miller seemed confused by her question. "He was staying with a friend. We're just waiting for his solicitor to arrive and then we'll question him."

"You've arrested him then?"

"Didn't have a lot of choice, really. We couldn't risk him doing another runner." There was the muffled sound of someone speaking in the background. "Got to go, the solicitor is here. I'll see you tomorrow." He hung up.

Could what Carl had done really be called a runner? Or was it simply that he had not told the police where he was currently staying out of innocent ignorance? After all, both the home he shared with his father and his mother's house were now crime scenes. Where did they expect him to stay? And then, once the police had pretty much named him as their primary suspect, he might have been too frightened to just surrender himself. Someone had probably done it for him, she thought, and would have liked to ask Miller this, but he had gone now, and he always switched his phone off in the interview room.

Callie wondered if Kate had been the next duty solicitor up. Having her best friend representing him would mean Carl got the best advice possible, but also that they wouldn't be able to talk about the case if Kate was involved.

With her concerns about Carl and Mrs Caldwell running around her mind, she knew sleep was not going to come easily. Perhaps some mindless late-night television would help? It was worth a try. But probably best to avoid the news channels, she thought as she reached for the remote.

Chapter 18

Callie woke the next morning, fully dressed on the sofa, with the television still on. She stretched and felt her joints protest that sofas were not the most comfortable places to sleep. She checked her watch, surprised to see that it was almost eight o'clock. She would need to get a move on if she was to get to work on time. Thank goodness the flat she was currently renting was only two floors up from the surgery, so the commute took no time at all.

At the end of surgery, Callie grabbed her list of visits and her bag, and headed off to the police station. She wanted to find out what had happened with Carl and whether Kate was his solicitor. Also, she could ask Jayne quietly what her next steps should be with Mrs Caldwell.

The main CID office was quiet when she got there, which was surprising given that they had three suspicious deaths to investigate, but she was relieved to see that Jayne was there, dressed in her usual combo of navy-blue chinos, flat shoes and a patterned shirt. Comfortable and practical, both for her work and home life, given that she had three small children. Callie had no idea how she coped, but registered that her wardrobe of patterned shirts rather than stain-showing white tops was a valuable part of her armoury.

"Hiya," Callie said as she came into the room. "Where is everyone?"

"Interview room, court, out looking for witnesses, off sick, on leave…" Jayne said, working her way around the room, pointing at each desk in turn.

"How is Carl's interview going?" Callie asked.

"Early days," Jayne replied with a shrug. "I know you don't think he's involved, but he must surely know why his family is being targeted, at the very least."

"Which is why arresting him and having him lawyer up and being advised to say 'no-comment' was a bad move," Callie responded. "He might have been more willing to co-operate if he was just brought in for an informal interview."

"Agreed, but he didn't want to do that," Jayne replied, not specifying which 'he' she was referring to, Miller or Carl. "And he hasn't requested legal advice."

Callie was surprised and relieved, as that meant Kate wasn't involved, yet. Knowing that she was unlikely to get more from Jayne on Carl's interview, she changed the subject to her other concern.

"What can I do if I have worries about a patient's welfare and social services don't feel they have enough time, staff or even evidence to intervene?" she asked.

"Not a lot," Jayne told her. "Why are you concerned? Do they seem in distress?"

"Well, I haven't actually been able to talk to her. I can't get past her carers."

"Oh, right. Difficult. But if her carers say she's fine, isn't that good enough for you?"

"That's just it," Callie answered, unable to keep the frustration out of her voice. "I have questions about the standard of care being delivered."

"What do their employers say?"

"It's a private arrangement."

"No relatives you can talk to?"

"None that I can find."

"Hmm, I can see why you are worried." Jayne thought for a moment. "Maybe Nigel could help you with finding any family – when he's back from leave, that is. You know how good he is with computer searches. He can find almost anyone. I have no idea how he does it."

"Me neither," said Callie, although the answer, she thought, was Nigel's unending patience. Both she and Jayne would give up checking lists of names and details long before he did.

"Other than that, you can keep trying to get past the carers and if they continue to block you, and social services agree, you could try asking uniform if they can go round and ask to talk to her, insist even, but, I'm warning you now, it's not going to be easy..." Jayne was distracted by the sound of angry voices in the corridor outside the office and the door flew open a few seconds later.

"This isn't the seventies, Bob, we had to stop the interview as soon as he said he wanted a solicitor," Miller said over his shoulder as he and Jeffries entered the room. It seemed like Jayne's 'yet' had come to pass. "Hello, er, Dr Hughes."

Everyone in CID knew that Callie and Detective Inspector Steve Miller were in a relationship, but Callie and Miller had agreed to keep things strictly professional at work, however hard that was at times, and everyone played along with that.

"Hello, Steve, I was just asking Jayne what I could do about that patient I am concerned about."

He didn't look like he knew what she was talking about.

"Oh, okay, well, we need to…" He indicated his office and looked meaningfully at his two detective sergeants.

"I'm just going." Callie took the hint and turned to Jayne. "Thanks for your help, I'll keep trying and maybe see if Nigel can track down a relative when he's back."

"Yeah, he's due back on Monday, I'm sure he will be able to do that for you."

Callie waved and went out, disappointed that Jayne hadn't really been any help on either front, but pleased that Carl had decided on legal advice, even if she crossed her fingers that that help wasn't Kate.

* * *

She is proving to be a much harder target, being teetotal, God-fearing and only going out to do good works or go to Bible meetings during the day. I've tried following her the last few evenings, hoping to catch her on her own, but there always seems to be someone around, a passer-by, a dog walker or a delivery van, someone who would see it if I made a move. And she's always tucked up safely in her own home – my home by rights – long before nightfall. Then, as soon as it's dark, she pulls the curtains and I can see nothing, nothing that will help me. This will be the riskiest one yet, but it's the order I planned and I don't want to change it, not now, not when I'm so close to fulfilment. It's a complication that the boy is in custody. They think he's the killer, and I don't want them realising their mistake just yet. I'll have to wait until he is out, then there will be another death they can pin on him.

Chapter 19

"Hi, Gauri, do you have a minute?" Callie had managed to catch the senior partner of her practice in the office before morning clinics had begun.

"Of course," Gauri Sinha replied, looking up from her laptop. "So long as you are not going to tell me you are leaving us, again."

In the last year, Callie had twice told Gauri she was leaving to go and live in Belfast with her then boyfriend Billy Iqbal, only to withdraw her resignation soon after. What could she say? The course of true love never did run smoothly? She was a commitment-phobe? Or, at the very least, indecisive? Even the calm, unflappable Gauri had begun to lose patience with the on-again, off-again move and the constant worry of finding a replacement for Callie.

"No, no, nothing like that. It's about a patient, Mrs Caldwell, Betty, lives on the Priory Estate," Callie hastily explained.

"Next door to Mr Herring, if I'm not mistaken."

"That's the one, yes."

Gauri quickly pulled up Mrs Caldwell's notes.

"She's not been seen for quite a while, but then, there's no history of any long-term conditions here, apart from a short note about her memory and that she was asked to come in for an assessment but… she doesn't seem to have come in for it…"

"No."

"Maybe she forgot," Gauri said with a slight smile.

"Quite, so when I visited Mr Herring, who also expressed some concerns about her, I knocked on her door, but there didn't seem to be anyone in and I left a note, asking her to call."

"But she didn't?"

"No, I tried calling but the phone number we have for her has been disconnected and her next of kin was listed as her husband, who died a while back."

"We really need to keep on top of these things." Gauri shook her head. "I'll ask Linda if we can get the office staff onto checking contact details of our elderly patients."

Linda, and the office team, were not going to thank her for making extra work for them but, equally, Callie thought it was important. The problem she was having with Mrs Caldwell had made that clear.

"Anyway, the next time I visited Mr Herring, I could hear someone was in at Mrs Caldwell's, so I knocked and asked to see her but her carers wouldn't let me in."

"Really?" Gauri was as surprised as Callie had been when it happened.

"They said she was asleep and they didn't want her disturbed."

Gauri frowned and clicked her tongue to show her disapproval.

"What firm are they from?" she asked.

"That's the problem, I've tried all of them and they say she isn't on their books. It seems to be a private arrangement. I've been to see Helen Austen but she's reluctant to do anything unless I can show that Mrs Caldwell is being mistreated or neglected."

"Which you can't do, if they won't let you in."

"Precisely."

There were a few moments of silence as both thought about what could be done.

"I can't just let it go," Callie said, forestalling what she felt sure Gauri was going to say.

"I understand, and deep down I know you are right to be worried. It doesn't sound right. You can go and ask to see her once again, but if they do not let you in, then I think you need to lean on your friendships, with the social worker and the police. Make them take notice – someone has to force their way in to be sure she is safe and well."

"Yes, I agree, Gauri, thank you." Callie was relieved she had approval for what she had already decided was her only option and as she went through the main office on her way to her own consulting room, Callie added Mrs Caldwell to her afternoon visit list.

* * *

It was Friday evening and The Crown was packed with people celebrating the end of the working week. Callie and Kate had found a corner table and squeezed in but were feeling a bit hemmed in, surrounded by people who were getting louder by the pint.

"So come on, tell me why you've had such a bad day?" Kate asked her once they were settled with their drinks in front of them.

"It's a long story," Callie said, taking a large sip from her wine glass.

"I've got all evening," Kate responded. "Is Carl still in custody?"

Callie had been relieved to discover that Kate was not the duty solicitor called in when Carl had asked for legal advice.

"They got a thirty-six-hour extension yesterday morning, but I don't think they will get another," Callie told her. "So he should be out by eleven tonight."

"They'll probably let him out earlier if they haven't got any evidence. Any solicitor worth their salt will have made sure of that."

"I hope he does have someone good, though I am pleased it's not you, for entirely selfish reasons."

"I know, it would have made life a bit difficult, wouldn't it? Even though we both agree the police are being a bit premature in arresting him."

"Agreed, but if he's not the killer, then at least they are keeping him safe from whoever it is, and I insisted he was put on suicide watch as I think that's a far more likely scenario."

"Bet they loved you for that." Kate laughed, and she was right.

Callie had seen the eye-roll from the custody sergeant when she had told him – it would have been hard to miss – but they both knew it would be much worse if Carl did kill himself while in custody, particularly after she had warned them of the possibility.

"I thought you said his alibis were checking out?" said Kate.

"I think they are, to a degree, but a bunch of drunken mates saying you were in the pub isn't exactly cast iron."

"CCTV?" Kate suggested.

"I'm sure they'll be checking it, but who knows how quickly, especially with Nigel on leave."

Kate knew DC Nigel Nugent was the go-to guy for anything his colleagues considered boring: analysing data, checking CCTV or going through vast quantities of text messages and photos from someone's mobile phone.

"I'm guessing you made your feelings known to a certain Detective Inspector?"

Callie grimaced at this question.

"Erm, yes," she replied.

"And he didn't take it well?"

Callie didn't comment, but her face said it all. Miller hadn't taken it well at all and he had told her, in no uncertain terms, to butt out of his business. What was worse, he'd said it in front of Bob Jeffries.

"He'll get over it," Kate told her firmly.

Callie knew she was right, Miller never seemed to sulk or hold a grudge for long. At least he hadn't so far. The problem was, Callie was not the same.

"If Carl isn't the killer and, like you, I'm certainly not convinced that he is, who can it be? I mean, the way you've described the situation, he does at least benefit from the deaths. Does anyone else?"

"Not that I am aware," Callie said. "I can only think that it isn't about the boat but rather, something about the family."

"But what? They seem a perfectly ordinary fishing family. I mean, are there any other people connected to them that you know about?"

"Well, there was the other man who worked with them, the crewman, um…" She wracked her brains for his name. "Des? Den? Yes, Denny, he was there when I went to the first death, comforting Carl." Callie thought for a moment. "Then there was the bloke who got into a fight with Jack

Porter, Carl's dad. He only had one arm, but that doesn't discount him and he certainly seemed to have some sort of a grievance."

"Has he been interviewed then?"

"Not yet as far as I know. Maybe I should say something to Steve to remind him. What do you think?"

"I think you should," Kate said, "only be prepared for him telling you to butt out again."

"No change there then. Anyway," Callie said firmly, "after I left the police station, I went back to try and see the patient I told you about. The lady whose carers wouldn't let me in earlier in the week."

"Any success?"

"Nope, no one even answered the door, even though I could hear them in there. Complete waste of time. Apart from seeing another patient of mine go in there after I had had no success."

"What?"

Callie recalled the scene as she described it to Kate. It had already been dark, with a light drizzle, and she was hunched in her raincoat under an umbrella, but she hadn't yet given up and headed back to her car. She was standing in the courtyard, looking up at the walkway and Mrs Caldwell's flat and wondering about what her next move should be, when some movement in the alley leading from the road caught her eye.

"It was Marcy," Callie told Kate. "Marcy Draper. You remember Marcy, don't you?"

"All too well," Kate said with a groan.

Marcy was a sex worker and a drug addict with a terrible temper. She was a regular customer of both Kate and Callie as client and patient.

"Did you speak to her?"

"She was moving too fast for me to catch her on her way in, but I was waiting for her when she came back down."

"And you are sure she went into your patient's flat?"

Business-like, as always, Kate was making absolutely sure of the quality of the evidence before giving her verdict. Callie loved her for that.

"Absolutely sure. I couldn't see what she did to get their attention, or what I had done differently, but the man opened the door. I can't be sure of exactly what happened from where I was standing, but after a few seconds, the door closed again and Marcy came down the stairs. I was waiting for her at the bottom. She nearly jumped out of her skin when I said her name."

"I can imagine." Kate laughed.

"I asked her what she had been doing at the flat."

"Although you must have had a good idea."

"Yes, I was pretty sure she had just bought some drugs."

"It could have been her other job, you know, maybe he was the client?"

"He didn't last long if so, she was only there a minute, if that." Callie smiled at the thought. "Anyway, she said she was just visiting old friends but her guilty look told me that wasn't true. She really wasn't keen to talk to me there so I took her down the road to a pub."

"And she told you they are dealing from the flat," Kate said.

"Exactly. Nothing heavy. Marcy had just bought some temazepam and said she didn't know anything about any old lady living there when I asked."

"So how come they let her in and not you? Do they have a secret knock or something?"

"Secure messaging. She texts in an order, they give her a time to collect, she texts again when she's at the door. They don't want to accidently answer the door to me or the social worker again, it seems."

"Understandable," Kate told her. "It's called cuckooing."

"What is?"

"When drug dealers take over the home of someone vulnerable. They get a free home with all the utilities, a secure place to deal from, and they are probably taking her money too."

It suddenly all made sense.

"It makes me so angry," said Callie.

"I agree. So, what are you going to do about it?" Kate knew her friend all too well, there was no way she was going to just leave it like that.

"I've formally requested both police and social work back-up for an enforced visit. I wanted it tomorrow, but Helen isn't on duty this weekend. She agreed to Monday morning when I had a bit of a tantrum."

"What about the police? I mean, it's a drug den. They should raid it."

"Steve said he wanted to do it properly, set up some surveillance first. I told him I can't wait for all that. Mrs Caldwell is vulnerable and we don't know what sort of condition she is in or if she is even still alive."

"What did he say to that?"

"He said I was being melodramatic." Tears sprang to Callie's eyes as she recalled the scene in his office.

Kate stroked her hand, understanding just how hard it must have been for her friend.

"So, we've agreed a compromise," Callie continued. "He's asked a couple of DCs to keep watch on the address over the weekend and will try and get a raid together for Monday if they see evidence of drug dealing."

"What if they don't see any signs of dealing?"

"Then Helen and I will have to go it alone."

Callie's call for help hadn't pleased either Steve or Helen. They had both pointed out that she was pushing her friendship with them to the limit, Callie remembered as she emptied her glass. In fact, they had both been more than a little exasperated with her, telling her all the reasons why it wasn't a good idea to rush in; that she needed to let the police handle it properly, or for a different social work department to make enquiries, but Callie had stuck to her guns. The other options would all take too long and she could use her relationships with the two of them to put the pressure on without causing too much of a rift. At least, she hoped she could.

"I'm going to see this woman Monday morning and you can help me gain entry or arrest me for breaking and entering," she had finally said to Miller as she stormed out of his office. She wondered if he'd forgive her for that. One thing was for sure, if he didn't help her to get some kind of police back-up, she wouldn't forgive him.

* * *

Friday night is bible study and fellowship at the rectory, led as usual by the vicar's wife. It finishes at eight, but the members always stay afterwards for coffee and biscuits. I know this because I have watched her closely over the last couple of weeks, so that I can be sure exactly where I will find her. I know that she will start out walking home with two or three others from the group, but that they will soon peel off and go their separate ways, and I am relieved that tonight they stick to their routine. As before, she has to walk the last bit of the route on her own.

I have also been watching the police station whenever I can and, as luck would have it, I was there when Carl appeared, accompanied by his solicitor, a scrawny little man in an ill-fitting suit. I knew the police would have to let him go soon; they really didn't have any evidence against him.

Poor boy, enjoy your freedom, it isn't going to last long.

Carl's release meant I was free to go back to my plan again and I hurried to where I knew I would find her, following the little group as they walk towards the houses on the hill. First one and then another saying their goodbyes and turning off until, by the time we reach the bottom of Langtry's Flight, the last set of steps on her way home, she is on her own. Well, apart from me, that is. She seems to have no idea that I am following her. I have been keeping well back as I don't want to spook her, but now she is alone, I have to catch her before she reaches the top and out onto the road where there is light. There is a camera on the side wall of the shop at the top of the steps as well, high up so I couldn't reach it. And there might be people walking along the road, or in the shop – witnesses. But I know the camera doesn't reach this far down, I looked at the video display in the shop when I went there last week. The only light, halfway up, is broken. I threw a stone at it several days ago, when I made my plan. Half the enjoyment is in the planning, making sure I have everything covered.

I run up the steps, two at a time, careful not to slip or make too much noise. I don't want to give her any warning, and she doesn't seem to hear me, doesn't feel the threat. Perhaps she believes that her god will protect her.

As I come up behind her, she turns and I see recognition in her eyes and a moment of fear as she sees the hammer in my hand and realises what I am about to do, but it doesn't last long. She is dead before she can cry out.

Chapter 20

"Who found her?" Callie asked as she rapidly donned her crime scene suit.

"A woman who lives on Priory Road. She was coming back from a night out," Sergeant Bracewell told her. They were standing at the top of the narrow steps that led down from Plynlimmon Road – Langtry's Flight. "I've left a constable with her because she was a bit shaken, as you can imagine."

"Must have sobered her up pretty quick. Do we know who the victim is?" She snapped on her second glove and was ready to approach the body.

"Haven't checked her bag yet," Bracewell said with a shake of his head. "Didn't want to touch anything until you and the CSIs have done your bit."

Nodding her approval, Callie clicked on her head torch. The street lamp here meant the top of the steps were brightly lit and she could see cameras fixed to the shop wall too, but the light didn't penetrate more than the first flight down. She started down the steps that ran between the shop and the houses and led down to St Mary's Terrace. She hadn't gone far before she could make out a body lying in a heap halfway down. There was another lamp post there but the light didn't seem to be working. Kneeling down next to the body, she saw that it belonged to a slight, grey-haired woman with her hair in a bun at the nape of her neck. She was wearing a beige raincoat over a woollen dress, thick tights that had miraculously stayed intact, and sensible, flat-heeled shoes. Callie noticed that the thin grey hair was escaping the pins meant to hold it in place and had red streaks from the blood that had pooled beneath her head. Callie could see at least one wound to the side of her cranium, which explained the streaks, but most of the destruction was to the victim's face, now an unrecognisable mush of blood and tissue. There was a real sense of anger to the injuries.

There was a piece of rope similar to the ones used in the earlier hangings lying beside the body, which made the hairs on the back of Callie's neck stand on end. Callie photographed the woman with her phone before moving the collar of the beige raincoat to one side. Sure enough, the rope was looped around the woman's neck, just like all the others, but, as with Marie Porter, it had not been pulled tight.

Callie sat back on her heels. What on earth was going on?

"Okay to take over?" a voice called out, and Callie looked up to see Colin Brewer and another CSI, suited and booted and ready to process the scene.

"All yours," she told him and stood up. Collecting her things and carefully retracing her route in, she moved back to the entrance of the steps.

She had signed out of the scene and was taking off her protective clothing when a car pulled up. It was Miller's. Bracing herself against the wall, she hurriedly finished pulling off her coverall as she heard the sound of two car doors slamming.

"What's up, Doc?" Jeffries asked.

"Elderly woman, face smashed in and a rope around her neck." Callie was unable to keep the tiredness from her voice. "Same type of rope as the others. At least you still have Carl in custody so you can rule him out."

Miller looked at Jeffries, who immediately turned and walked back to their car, pulling out his phone as he did so.

"Are you thinking this is a copycat or something?" she asked Miller.

"Obviously I can't rule that out, but Carl can't have killed her. We let him go at six o'clock last night," Miller told her quietly. "We weren't going to get another extension and his brief was pushing for us to let him go, so…"

Callie groaned.

"Yes, but why kill this woman? She can't be a member of his family, they're all dead."

Miller shrugged.

"Maybe he has other reasons," he said. "But we'll have to pull him in again, you've got to understand that."

"I suppose so," Callie said between gritted teeth. "But I still think you are making a big mistake concentrating all your efforts on him."

Chucking her used, crumpled-up overalls into the bin bag that was placed by the entrance to the scene for that purpose, Callie got into her car, slammed the door and drove off.

* * *

"Ugh! What time is it?" Kate slurred into the phone.

"Sorry, it's six thirty," Callie told her. "I just needed to talk to someone."

"What's he done now?"

Callie could hear a rustle as her friend sat up in bed. "He's totally fixated about Carl being the killer, even though this latest corpse can't be part of his family?"

"Which latest corpse?" Kate sounded instantly more awake.

"There was another murder last night. Elderly lady, face smashed in but there was a rope around her neck just like Marie Porter."

"Isn't Carl in custody? How can they think it was him?"

"He was released yesterday evening, so now, of course, they've gone straight round to his home to arrest him again."

"Oh God. Do you know who his counsel is?"

"No, but I can find out."

"Whoever it is, they can't be bad if they got him released."

"No." There were a few moments silence as they both thought about it.

"Wait a minute," Kate suddenly said. "It's a Saturday."

"Yes," Callie cautiously said.

"It's a Saturday so I don't have to work today. I can have a lie in."

"Oh. Sorry, I couldn't get back to sleep and I needed to offload."

"Well, you can offload all you like over a quick brunch at the café before I head up to London to see Sam. Eleven o'clock as usual, but for now, I'm going back to sleep. Bye!" Kate put the phone down.

Callie couldn't really blame her. She had forgotten that it wasn't a workday, but there was no way she was going to get any sleep. She had tried, tossing and turning in her bed since she returned from the crime scene, but her brain insisted on going round and round with it all. Was the latest victim a previously unknown family member? Or was she the victim of a copycat killer and nothing to do with the Porter family at all? If so, what details had been released to the public? Could anyone have known about the type of rope used in every case, or was it just so ubiquitous in the fishing world that everyone had some of it lying around? And, most importantly, did Carl have a cast-iron alibi this time?

She had so many questions and very few answers. There was nothing for it; she was going to have to go to the police station and see if she could find out what was going on.

* * *

"Hiya," Callie said as she entered the incident room. Unlike on her last visit, the room was a hive of activity, as more desks were being brought in and set up under Jayne's supervision.

"Hiya," Jayne replied. "Heard you had a disturbed night."

"Yes, another one." Callie nodded in the direction of a civilian worker who was busy plugging in extra phones. "The DI has decided to run this as a full-scale incident, has he?"

"Yes, well, with four deaths now, and the last two categorically suspicious – no matter how much he and the super tried to explain away the first two – there was no choice."

Jayne looked as if she agreed with Callie that this should have been done earlier, but they both knew it wasn't just Miller's call. The superintendent would have been keen to avoid the extra cost that a major investigation inevitably meant.

"I think we are agreed that all four are suspicious now," Callie told her and looked towards Miller's office. It was empty. "Is Steve interviewing Carl?"

"He wishes," Jayne said. "They're all still out looking for him."

"He wasn't at home?"

"No, we released his dad's house after the CSIs had finished and he went there, that's for sure, but he must have turned around and left pretty quickly. It looks like he's taken a load of stuff with him. Clothes, laptop, games console, all the essentials for a teenager on the run. Oi, you!" Jayne turned to a woman who had unceremoniously dropped an armful of extension leads in the middle of the room. "Those need to be given to him." She pointed to a man who was busy sorting out wiring for the extra desks. The woman sighed and gave Jayne a disgruntled look, but she picked up the leads again and took them over to where she had been asked to. Jayne hurried over to give further instructions on how they were to be used.

Left to her own devices, Callie wandered over to the whiteboard at the front of the room where before and after pictures of all the victims were displayed, including the latest. Callie was surprised to see that the woman pictured was familiar from somewhere. She checked the name written under the before picture. Rose Hudson.

"Yeah, this latest one doesn't seem to be connected." Jayne was standing behind Callie's shoulder, looking at the board as well.

"She is, you know," Callie told her. "At least, if she's who I think she is, she's definitely connected, if only by marriage. I saw her and Marie Porter having an argument by the net shops," she turned to Jayne. "Just after Simon Porter's death."

Chapter 21

Over brunch, Kate had not been surprised to hear that the latest victim was yet another member of the Porter-Hudson extended family, if only because she was once married to Harry Hudson and contributed her name to his half of the RoseMarie. There hadn't been much of a chance to discuss this latest addition to the death register as Kate wanted to get away and see Sam so, once she had left, Callie headed to the hospital. It might be a weekend but she wanted to know more about this latest victim.

She walked down the corridor towards the autopsy suite and then poked her head around the door of the empty office. She tutted at the untidiness and turned towards the door opposite just as Jim slammed it open with a dirty laundry hopper.

"Geez, Dr Hughes, you made me jump," Jim said with a laugh. "If you are looking for Matt or Dr Iqbal, they're inside giving the latest body a once over."

"Thanks, Jim." Callie hoped her face didn't display her anxiety at the news that Billy was there as well. She was being ridiculous, she told herself. She might have been in a relationship with Billy for two years but they had split up, or rather, she had split with him after she had discovered his affair with another GP while he was living in Belfast. She didn't flatter herself that he had come back to the area to be near her – after all, he hadn't even let her know he had left Northern Ireland. Miller was probably right, it was more likely that he had heard of a permanent job going in the south of England and had returned to be nearer his family.

She made her way through the lobby which had changing rooms, sluice, and equipment stores leading off it and went into the main room used for post-mortems. Matt Baxter and Billy both looked up and smiled as she came in.

"Welcome," Matt said. "This one's a bit of a mess." He gestured at the body she had last seen on the steps.

"I know, bit different from the others, isn't she?" Callie braced herself and looked at the face of the poor woman. It was no prettier now than it had been the night before. In fact, with some of the blood washed away to make the wounds clearer, the damage looked even worse. "The violence is escalating," she said.

"That is for sure," Matt said.

"Yes," said Billy, as he looked down at the woman. "It's a worrying trend."

"Or is it just that this one victim has been subjected to more violence for some reason?" Callie asked him.

"No, I think it's a clear progression. Victim one was drugged and hanged; victim two was drugged and probably died of an unintended overdose, with the hanging being done post-mortem; victim three was beaten, manually strangled and then hanged; and this poor lady, well, she was hit multiple times with what I suspect was a hammer and then just had the rope put round her neck."

"Why didn't he strangle her?"

"I've only done a preliminary drug wipe and blood alcohol test, but she was the first victim who would seem to have been sober and drug-free. All the others were severely impaired. Perhaps he was worried about her fighting back?"

"She's only small," Callie said. "She couldn't have put up that much of a fight."

"The killer might not be very big, or physically strong enough to be sure of overpowering her."

"Or they could be a woman," Matt added.

Callie didn't want to think about a woman being responsible for the four deaths, but she knew she shouldn't discount the possibility.

"The rope has to mean something to the killer," Callie said. "They add it even when they haven't used one to kill the victim."

"Symbolic?" Matt suggested.

"Of what?" she asked.

Matt shrugged.

"Hanging was used in cases of capital punishment," Billy told them both.

"Yes, but that was years ago," Callie said.

"Capital punishment was abolished here in 1969 but not until 1973 in Northern Ireland," Billy told her. "That isn't very long ago at all."

"And there's plenty of people who would like to see it brought back," Matt added.

Callie hated to think the deaths were a form of punishment, but it made a sick sort of sense.

"The other worrying aspect is the move away from specific targets, in that the others were all in one family," Billy said.

"I'm not so sure the killer has moved away from the family," she told them. "I believe this woman was married to Jack Porter's deceased business partner. Hopefully I'll know for sure later."

Billy looked at her in a way she recognised from their time together. It was a look that meant that he would like to tell her to be careful and not investigate anything herself, but it also conveyed that he knew she wouldn't appreciate him saying that, so he would keep quiet. She wished that Steve Miller had learned that look; instead, he never failed to tell her to stop interfering in his investigations and they had had more than a few rows about it now. Particularly over this case.

"Anyway, will you let me know if anything crops up in the PM?" she asked Billy.

"Of course." He grinned. "Am I allowed to let the police know first?"

"If you have to." She grinned back and was still smiling when she got into her car. Billy always knew how to make her smile, unlike a certain detective inspector.

* * *

Callie would have liked to have taken Kate along to The London Trader with her, but her friend had hurried off as soon as they'd finished their brunch and wasn't planning to return until late the next day, and Callie didn't want to wait.

As Callie pushed the door open, she was immediately struck by how much busier the pub was on a Saturday than a weekday. Looking round she was relieved to see that Old George was sitting at his usual table, nursing a nearly empty pint glass. Callie wondered if he had actually left his seat at all in the intervening hours and days. He certainly looked to be still wearing the same clothes. She sincerely hoped that he had been home since her last visit, if only to change his underwear.

"Hello, George," Callie said as she put a fresh pint in front of him. "Do you mind if I join you?"

"I never object to a lady's company," he told her, before adding, "especially when they bring beer." He quickly emptied his own glass and pulled the new one towards him, as if afraid she would take it away again. "Where's your friend, the one with the big…" He gestured towards his chest.

"She's elsewhere today," Callie said, with a slightly fixed smile. "I wondered if I could ask you a few questions?"

"Course," he replied. "I can tell you a few stories about my time on the boats, back in the day—"

"I really want to talk about the RoseMarie," she said. "About the ownership back in the beginning, when she was bought. You said that Harry Hudson and Jack Porter bought her and named it after their wives."

"That's right, Marie Porter, she was a right looker she was, but it was Rose what put up the money for them to buy it. She came from money that one, not that she looked like it brought her any happiness. Sour-faced bi—"

"So, Rose bought the boat but it was registered in Harry and Jack's names?" Callie asked.

"That's right, and Jack paid her back for his half over time," he responded, looking expectantly at his already empty glass.

Callie grabbed it and went to the bar to fetch him another.

"So," she resumed once he had his fresh pint, "when Harry died…" She paused. "When was that exactly? When Harry died?"

"Must be three years ago now, seems like yesterday."

"So his share in the boat would have gone back to Rose, as his wife, wouldn't it? But you said it went to Jack?"

George thought for a moment.

"I do remember there was a bit of a whatsit about that. Argument."

"So you said before." She gently tried to nudge his memory.

"It were a while ago, there was something right odd about it, now what was it?" He rubbed his chin as he thought. "I can remember things from way back when, but more recent things…"

Callie kept quiet whilst he thought, willing him to remember.

"It were something about Harry leaving his share to his son," George said eventually.

"I thought you said Harry and Rose didn't have any children?"

"They didn't have any with Rose, like, no, but Harry was a bit of a lad, if you know what I mean. Probably had kids all over the place." George chuckled and winked at Callie.

"So, you think he left his share of the boat to an illegitimate son?"

"A bastard son, that's right. I'm sure of it. Well, pretty sure."

"But you thought he'd left it to Jack before?"

"Hmm, maybe. I can't quite put me finger on it." He was tapping his finger against his glass, which was nearly empty, again, but Callie wasn't going to buy him another, not when his memory was so unreliable.

"Jack or an illegitimate son?" she pressed, but he just shrugged.

"You should ask Denny," he finally said. "He didn't join the crew until later, but he might know. He worked with 'em for two or three years, after all," he said before continuing with less certainty. "Or was it after Old Harry died that he started with 'em?" He thought for a moment before shaking his head. "Dunno. Coulda been just before or just after." And his glass was magically empty again.

After buying him one last pint, he had tried to help after all, Callie left him to his beer.

* * *

"How do I go about finding the contents of a will?" Callie said as soon as Kate picked up the phone.

"That depends – has it been through probate?"

"I should imagine so; it was a couple of years ago now. Possibly three. My source's memory isn't as good as it should be."

"Haha, I can imagine who that was then. Maybe you shouldn't have bought him so much beer."

"Tell me about it. So how do I set about finding out?"

"That's easy if it was an English will, anyway. It's a public record and you can go online and search for it on the gov.uk website, and order a copy. It's not even that expensive."

"Great, thanks, I'll do that then. I'll be able to find out when exactly he died from the death register, which will help."

"Yes and no. You have to search under the year probate was granted rather than the year of death, as far as I remember. That sometimes causes problems if probate took a while – you know, because it was challenged or something."

"I think this one might well have been, so I'll bear that in mind, thanks."

"That's good. Hope it goes well. Let me know how you get on and if you find the will you're looking for. I could maybe help with that tomorrow evening if you haven't got anywhere."

"Cheers, Kate. That might be really helpful and it would be good to catch up. Bye!"

Callie put the phone down and checked her watch. She had already walked past the RoseMarie on her way home after talking to George, but there had been no sign of Denny there or at the net shops. She would have another go at finding him tomorrow, but he might well be taking the weekend off, and who could blame him? Meanwhile she could follow Kate's advice and check out the government website, unless Steve Miller had replied to her earlier text suggesting dinner.

She checked her messages, and he had. She quickly opened the message, but it said he was too busy tonight. There was a sorry and one 'x'. Callie was going to be spending another night in on her own. Just her, her thoughts and the search for Harry Hudson's will.

Chapter 22

"Have you heard from Nigel? Has he been able to find any relatives of your Mrs Caldwell?" Kate asked early on Monday morning. She had phoned just as Callie was about to head out of the door.

"He only got back from his holiday this morning and has already run a quick search, bless him. There was no one he could find but he'll take another look."

"And the watch on the flat?"

"A few people came and went, but not enough to warrant a raid, according to a certain Detective Inspector."

"Not even in exchange for sexual favours?"

"No, not even then." Callie laughed at the suggestion, but the fact was, she hadn't seen Steve Miller in person over the weekend and had barely spoken to him, or even texted. She had to laugh or she would cry. She had had to get most of her information from others on his team. She had spent the Saturday night applying for a copy of Harry's will and then having a long soak in the bath and an early night. Sunday had been a day for walking along the beach where there was still no sign of Denny, followed by Sunday lunch at her parents, fending off questions about why Steve wasn't with her and why he hadn't proposed yet.

"You aren't going to storm the flat on your own, I hope?" Kate asked.

"No, no. Don't worry. Jayne stepped in and persuaded the duty sergeant to send a couple of uniforms. They should meet me there in about an hour's time, and Helen has promised to be there too," Callie told Kate.

"Well, let me know how it goes, I should be out of court by lunchtime."

Callie promised she would, and decided she had just about enough time for a coffee and croissant at the café before heading to Mrs Caldwell's, provided she resisted the temptation to pop into the surgery.

* * *

As she pulled up in the road near the flats, Callie was pleased to see that a marked police car was already there waiting. She got out of her car and went over to it, looking for a sign of Helen's car, but no matter where she looked it definitely wasn't there.

Abi Adeola got out of the police car along with a strapping young lad that Callie didn't know. She heaved a sigh of relief. Abi was good with people but if things got physical Callie would be very pleased to have the young man's muscle there to help. From what she had seen of the two youngsters caring for Mrs Caldwell, they wouldn't be too much of a handful for him.

"Hi, Abi, thanks for helping me out," Callie said.

"That's okay, what exactly is the problem? The sarge wasn't too clear."

"It's a patient of mine whose unofficial carers have refused me entry so that I check on her."

"Unofficial?" the male constable queried.

"Yes, they are not employed by any of the care firms locally, and no one has been unable to find any family members who might have employed them."

"Could the patient have employed them herself?"

"Of course, but then she would be able to confirm that if they let me in to speak to her, so why won't they?"

The two PCs looked at each other.

"It does sound a bit iffy," Abi said. "What's the patient's name?"

"Mrs Caldwell."

"And social services don't have any record?"

"No." Callie saw a white Smart car pull up and park in an impossibly small space. "I think that's the social worker now. I asked that they send someone so we are covered on all fronts."

The two constables looked relieved and Callie turned back to them.

"I just want to be sure that she's okay and if she is, we'll just leave them to it."

"Okay," Abi said.

Helen hurried over to them, slightly out of breath. "Sorry I'm late – are we ready to go? Only I've got to be somewhere at twelve."

They walked across the courtyard to Mrs Caldwell's block. They could hear loud music as they approached the stairs up to the first floor.

"I think we can safely say they're in," Callie said.

"Blimey, you'd think the neighbours would complain," Abi commented.

"I think they have," Callie told her. "But the carers, or whatever they are, threatened anyone who spoke up, so they've all stopped."

"Will you two be going in first?" Helen asked the police officers anxiously.

"We only have a back-up role here, so it's probably best if you or Dr Hughes knock and ask to see the patient first. If they refuse, then we can insist."

Helen didn't look happy.

"It's okay," Callie said. "I'll knock and ask to see her, Helen. I doubt they'll refuse if they see I'm not alone."

The social worker didn't look convinced by Callie's argument.

"Neither of them is that big, I doubt they'd want to take on anyone the size of the constable here."

Said constable grimaced and looked at his partner.

"Don't hesitate to call for back-up if it gets a bit tasty," he said.

Callie went up to the door, Helen standing well behind her and the two constables slightly to one side. She pushed the bell and knocked once, and when there was no response, knocked again, harder.

Mr Herring opened his front door, glanced at them and quickly closed it again. Callie heard the locks and bolts being put on as he secured himself inside his own property. He certainly wasn't going to come out and help.

Callie knocked again.

"Hello? Can you open the door please?" She shouted and was rewarded by the music being turned down. She knocked again and heard a whispered conversation going on behind the locked door.

"Who is it?"

"It's Dr Hughes. I've come to see Mrs Caldwell."

"She don't want to see you. She told us to tell you to leave her alone."

"She needs to tell me that herself."

"Her social worker says she doesn't need to see you, so go away."

"Really, I have her social worker here as well. She also wants to see Mrs Caldwell. Now open the door."

There were a few minutes of silence.

"This is harassment. She don't want to see either of you. Go away before I call the police!"

With a sigh, Abi took over from Callie.

"This is the police and we are here to do a welfare check, as there are serious concerns as to the well-being of Mrs Caldwell. Now please, open the door and let the doctor and social worker in to check on her, or we will have to force entry."

There was no immediate response.

"Permission needed to force entry to flat 21, Aiken Building, Whitecroft Estate, for an urgent check on the welfare of an elderly, vulnerable female," Abi spoke loudly into her radio, making sure that the people inside the flat would be able to hear.

There was a short, muttered conversation behind the door and then footsteps hurriedly going away, followed by some bangs.

"They're doing a runner!" Abi shouted. "Round the back, Joe." Her colleague was already on his way. "Back-up needed at Whitecroft Estate, suspects doing a runner," she added into her radio, as she hurried after Joe who was already halfway down the stairs.

Callie and Helen looked at each other.

"What do we do now?" Helen asked.

"Good question," Callie answered before having an idea. She went to the next door and knocked. "Mr Herring? It's Dr Hughes. Can you open the door, please?"

There was the sound of bolts and locks being opened and Mr Herring appeared at the door.

"I saw them. They climbed down from the balcony and ran away. There were two police officers chasing them."

"I know," Callie said. "We need to get into the flat to check on Mrs Caldwell. Do you still have a key?"

He hesitated.

"I won't tell anyone you gave it to me," she reassured him, "and I don't think they'll be back anyway." She crossed her fingers.

"Of course." Mr Herring took a steadying breath and quickly fetched a box of keys from the kitchen and sorted through them, picking one out. "Here. It can be a bit sticky, so you have to jiggle it round a bit."

Callie took the key and went back to where Helen was standing waiting. "Right, let's see what's been going on," she said.

Nothing could have prepared Callie for the state of the flat as she went in. The kitchen was piled high with dirty dishes and takeaway cartons. There were overflowing ashtrays everywhere and signs of drug-taking in amongst the empty bottles and cans in the living room.

"Don't touch anything," Callie warned Helen.

"Not a chance," Helen replied with a grim smile. "Not without a hazmat suit." She looked around. "Where's the bedroom?"

"Through here." Callie led the way towards the main bedroom door and braced herself before opening it. The curtains were drawn, making it hard to see anything in the dim light from the hallway. There was an overpowering smell of urine and faeces. Holding her hand over her nose, Callie went to the window and opened the curtains. There was a sharp intake of breath behind her as she did so and she turned to see Helen, looking shocked and staring at the bed. Now that she had enough light to see, Callie went over to her patient. Mrs Caldwell, frail and emaciated to the point of being cadaverous, was lying on her back, eyes closed, mouth open, dried saliva tracks on her chin. She was deathly pale and very still. So still, in fact, that Callie thought she was dead until she grasped her patient's hand and detected a faint, fluttering pulse.

Opening her doctor's bag, Callie took out a stethoscope.

"Mrs Caldwell? Can you hear me?" She gave the old lady a slight shake without response and, opening the front of the stained night dress, listened to her chest for a moment before turning to Helen. "Can you call for an ambulance please, Helen. Tell them it's an emergency."

Helen hurried out into the hallway and Callie could hear her on the phone to the emergency services.

Mrs Caldwell looked severely dehydrated and Callie took an assortment of equipment out of her medical bag to try and start intravenous fluids, but she was struggling to find a vein anywhere that would take a cannula.

"They want to know if she's breathing," Helen called from the hallway.

"Yes, just," Callie replied, "but she's unconscious and not responding."

Callie pulled back the bed clothes and continued to look for a patent vein, trying to ignore the fact that Mrs Caldwell was lying in such soiled linen. Finally succeeding in getting a butterfly cannula into her patient's foot, Callie slowly administered a bolus of IV dextrose-saline. She had some large bags of sterile fluids in the back of her car, but didn't want to leave Mrs Caldwell. If the ambulance didn't arrive quickly, she'd send Helen down for them.

"It's going to be all right, Mrs Caldwell, help is on the way," she told her patient, hoping she was right and that it wasn't already too late.

* * *

Callie was exhausted by the time she got back to her home. She sat in the chair by the window, staring out at the sea and thinking about the day.

Abi Adeola and her colleague Joe had arrived back at Mrs Caldwell's flat just as the ambulance was leaving. They had lost the two runners in the maze of alleys, she explained. The suspects had had too much of a head start to make their capture and apprehension possible. Abi could see how frustrated Callie was by the thought that they might have got away with it all, and had hastened to reassure her that they were bound to have left enough forensic clues to be identified.

"We'll get them, don't you worry," the constable had told her, but Callie wasn't sure they would. A brief inspection of the rear balcony at the flat had revealed a rope already tied to the railings in preparation for a quick escape. The couple were clearly cunning enough to have survived this far and would know that they needed to make themselves scarce. They were probably well on their way to London by now.

She had followed Mrs Caldwell to the hospital only to get more depressing, if not unexpected, news. Mrs Caldwell was in a very bad way; her kidneys had shut down because of severe dehydration. She also had chronic infections in the many bedsores she had developed from lying in her own mess for so long. The young houseman wasn't hopeful that the patient would recover or would even make it through the night.

Callie knew in her heart that he was probably right. She had sat with her patient, holding her hand and talking to her for a while, but had finally admitted that she was exhausted, and headed home.

Now, in the comfort of her chair on the balcony looking out over the net shops to the sea, invisible in the dark, and listening to the restful sound of the waves on the shore, she closed her eyes and was asleep in seconds.

* * *

The next day, Callie sat in the office, munching a tasteless tuna sandwich, wondering why she didn't go upstairs and make herself something nicer for lunch; then remembered that there wasn't anything in the cupboards because she hadn't been shopping. Taking another bite of the claggy supermarket bread, she started thinking about how she could find out who would now own the RoseMarie and what she was worth.

Had either Jack or Simon made a will? If not, Jack's share of the boat would presumably have been divided between Simon and Carl, but as Simon had died first, would his share go to Carl? Or half to Sharon? And if the boat was the motive, why kill Rose Hudson? And what about Marie Porter? She had nothing to leave anyone either.

No, these murders were not about gain, she thought. It was much more likely they were about revenge, but she just couldn't think who would want revenge on a whole family and anyone connected to them. Surly Dick, as the other fishermen seemed to call the one-armed Richard Simmons, seemed the most likely person, in her opinion, but again, why kill Rose and Marie?

Nothing seemed to make any sense and her mind kept going back to Mrs Caldwell. Her condition had still been reported as critical by the ward sister when Callie had rung earlier.

Chucking the remains of her sandwich in the bin, Callie grabbed her bag and went out, calling to Linda as she passed her office.

"I'm going to the hospital to see how Mrs Caldwell is doing."

As she continued down the corridor to the stairs, she thought she heard Linda reply, "There is such a thing as a telephone, you know," but she might have been mistaken.

In the High Dependency Unit where Mrs Caldwell was being treated, the beds were spaced further apart than on other wards, to make room for the plethora of equipment needed. Callie checked the board and saw that her patient had been placed in a corner bed and the curtains drawn around her space. Callie pulled the curtain slightly to one side and saw a staff nurse busy detaching the heart monitor leads. The nurse looked up guiltily as Callie entered and stopped what she was doing.

"Dr Hughes," the nurse said quietly.

Callie turned to her patient and could see that the old woman was lying very still, pale and slack-mouthed. She didn't need to be a doctor to know that her patient was dead.

"I'm sorry—" the nurse started to say before Callie interrupted her.

"I think you should leave the electrodes and lines in place. Leave her absolutely as she is." The nurse looked startled by her outburst and Callie took a moment to compose herself and explain. "At the very least, this will be a coroner's case and if I have anything to do with it, it will be part of a criminal investigation. A murder investigation."

The nurse hurried away to get advice from someone more senior and Callie went up to the bed and took Mrs Caldwell's hand.

"I'm very sorry I didn't get to you earlier," she told the silent corpse. "But I promise I will make sure the people who did this to you pay for it."

Chapter 23

Callie had concentrated on her work at the surgery for a couple of days, trying not to think about how she might have saved Mrs Caldwell if she had forced her way into the flat earlier. The fact that she would not have had any support didn't make her feel any less guilty. Nigel had been unable to find any relatives, no one to mourn the old lady, no one who could blame her for her death, other than herself. Constantly beating herself up meant that she barely gave any thought to Carl and the Porter and Hudson families.

That evening, when she had got home from surgery, clutching the mail she had collected from her letter box in the lobby, she almost consigned everything into the recycling bin before she saw that amongst the usual junk mail there was a reply from the probate registry.

Callie tore open the envelope and read the information it held inside. Then read it again. She picked up the phone to call Kate.

"Hiya, do you have a moment?"

"For you? Of course. What's up?"

"I just got a copy of the will I asked for in the post and it's thrown me a bit."

"In a good way?"

"I really don't know. Let me read this bit out." Callie shuffled the papers to find the sentence she needed. "I hereby leave my share in the Hudson Porter Ltd business and the fishing boat RoseMarie to my only son, Simon Porter."

"So, Jack Porter left his boat to his son… hey, wait a bit, didn't he have two sons? Why does it say 'only son'?"

"Jack Porter did have two sons, or thought he did, but I haven't got a copy of *his* will, always supposing he even had one, as that would still be going through probate. No, this is Harry Hudson's will from three years ago."

There was a moment's silence as Kate took that in.

"Wow! Way to go. Announce you've cheated on your wife, cuckolded your best mate and business partner, and tell him his eldest son isn't actually his, all in one fell swoop. You have to admit, he's got style."

"I kept thinking about where I might have seen Rose Hudson before and then I remembered it was on the fishermen's beach by the net shops just after Simon had

died. She was arguing with Marie Hudson, I'm sure of it. I
didn't know who they were at the time. They were
shouting at each other and I nearly went over to them in
case it got out of hand."

"No surprises there. I can't imagine they'd be on
friendly terms after that level of infidelity, even if it was a
long time ago."

"And it's no wonder the Porter family fell apart and
Jack took to the bottle after Harry died and the will was
read."

"I'd probably have killed Harry if I was married to
him," Kate said.

"If he wasn't already dead."

"Very true. But it must have been a shock to find out
just how much of a shit he was."

"Exactly. Even I have to admit that it might be enough
to send someone crazy."

"Yes, but crazy enough to kill everyone concerned?"

That was the question, and Callie didn't have an
answer.

* * *

Callie and Miller had called an uneasy truce, so she
didn't ring him with the news about the will but waited for
him to arrive that evening as planned, which he did, late
and with his usual array of Indian takeaway food. There
were containers of pilau rice, lamb pasanda, butter chicken
masala, onion bhajis and keema naan, all packed tightly in
a paper carrier bag.

Even though it smelt delicious and Callie liked all of it,
she was beginning to long for something different. Fish
and chips maybe? Kebab? Or even Thai, just for a change.
She loved Thai food and she couldn't avoid it forever just
because it had been Billy's favourite.

Miller had brought beer for himself as well but not
wine, and Callie was exhausted, so she was sipping fizzy
water, feeling virtuous and wishing she could make herself

like the taste of beer. Maybe she should try it again? Perhaps it was an acquired taste. Kate had certainly acquired it.

"Have you found Carl yet?" Callie asked as she unpacked the bag.

"No."

She got out knives, forks and mango chutney, and Miller was piling food on his plate before she had finished.

"And is your latest victim, Mrs Hudson, definitely the wife of the late Harry Hudson? Co-owner of the RoseMarie?"

"Yup."

"You think they are all connected?"

"Yes."

Miller was busy eating and by the look of how quickly he was shovelling the food in, he seemed ravenous, but his monosyllabic answers were irritating her, so she persisted.

"And you still think Carl is behind all the deaths then?"

"Definitely."

Four syllables were a step in the right direction, she thought.

"Why? Why not someone else?"

"Who benefits? The list is getting smaller and ooh, look, Carl's still on it."

Callie would have preferred the terse responses than this sarcasm, but she wasn't about to let it drop.

"Have you seen Harry Hudson's will?" She gave him the copy that had arrived in the post. "Simon already owned half the RoseMarie, so Sharon presumably gets his half, not Carl. Do you seriously think that someone out there has killed four people just to own a boat, or rather, half of one?"

Miller carefully read the contents of Harry's will then dropped it on the table and returned to his food.

"That doesn't change things. Unless you seriously believe Sharon killed her husband a matter of weeks before she's due to give birth, just to get her hands on half a boat."

"Stranger things have happened, but I agree it's unlikely, simply because of the physical strength involved in the first three murders. I'm just saying the motive might not be the boat, but if it is, Sharon and the children might be in danger now."

"They've gone away – staying at her mum's for a bit, I think," Miller told her. "Just in case."

"Good." Callie was relieved to hear it. "Have you spoken to the bloke with one arm again? Richard Simmons?"

"Yes, and I'm not sure he could physically have committed these crimes either, no matter how angry he is at the family."

"Why exactly is he so angry?"

"Well, it all goes back to the accident that led to him losing his arm, apparently."

"I guessed as much."

"Quite. He says that Simon was still too inexperienced to be in charge of the winch when it happened but that Jack was training him up and reckoned he was." He nodded at the will lying on the table. "Must've been before the shit hit the fan with that. Anyway, the boat lurched and the net slipped, Simmons grabbed it, but his coat got caught on the rope and his arm was pulled into the winch."

Callie shuddered of the thought of seeing your arm being pulled into the machinery and being unable to stop it.

"He says he was shouting at Simon to shut it off, but he froze," Miller said.

"You can understand his anger."

"I know, but he sued for compensation and lost because they said it was him who had left the guard off the winch, not Simon, so he got some compensation but not as much as he wanted."

"Do you think it was him? Or did Jack and Simon just say that to reduce liability?"

Miller shrugged.

"Who knows." He put down his fork and reached for the naan bread. "Look. Can we stop talking about the case? I need a break, to get away from it, just for a moment, please?"

They continued to eat in an awkward silence. It was Miller who caved in first.

"Have you heard any more from the coroner about Mrs Caldwell?"

Little did he know that she had thought of nothing else for the last two days, up until she had read the will, and now he was pushing her right back to where she had been.

"He's opened the inquest and adjourned it until he has statements from the hospital doctors and there's been a PM. I think he's waiting to see if you catch the two of them." Callie was unable to keep the bitterness out of her voice.

"I know," he said. "And we will get them, I promise you."

"Those bastards must have just left her, lying in her own filth, for weeks." Callie rarely swore, but she really couldn't think of any other words to use for Mrs Caldwell's so-called carers. "Did the crime scene team find anything to identify who they were?"

"Yes, well, I'm not sure we've had the forensic report back yet."

Callie gave him an incredulous look, so he hurried on. "There were a variety of credit cards, all for different names; most had been reported lost or stolen when Nigel checked with the owners."

"Kate said it's not uncommon for drug dealers to take over the flat of a vulnerable person."

"Cuckooing, yes," Miller said.

"But you will have enough to charge them when you find them?"

"Absolutely. As well as the credit cards, they found a few pills, some powder and weed, plus weighing scales and a number of the little bags they use, so they were definitely dealing from the flat. It's a wonder there weren't more complaints from the neighbours."

"I think they did a pretty good job of intimidating anyone who spoke out."

"I can imagine." Miller wiped his plate clean with naan bread.

"I hope you catch them and throw them into jail for a very long time," Callie said. "What they did was absolutely bloody despicable." She couldn't keep the slight tremor out of her voice as she thought about the terrible state she had found Mrs Caldwell in. "I just wish I'd forced my way in sooner."

Miller pushed his plate away and took her hand.

"You can't blame yourself for this. Any other doctor wouldn't have forced their way in the way you did, and the old lady would have been found dead months later when we finally raided the place."

"She's still dead."

"Yes, but you very nearly saved her."

Callie sniffed and allowed herself to be pulled into a long, comforting hug, which led onto an embrace, and a lingering kiss.

"Let's forget the washing up and have an early night," Miller suggested.

And just this once, Callie thought he was probably right. The clearing up could wait.

* * *

I can't find him anywhere. Not in the pubs, not with his mates. No one's seen him and I can't risk asking around too much in case it raises anyone's suspicions. He must have gone into hiding. I'm not surprised. Young Carl always was the brightest of the bunch, clever enough to hate fishing and clever enough to work out that someone is killing off his family, it seems. But I'll find him, or the police will do it for me. He's got to surface sometime. He's a Hastings boy, there's no way he'll be able to stay away forever.

Chapter 24

The next morning, Callie seriously regretted her decision not to clear up properly and just leave everything piled in the sink. The smell of stale curry and beer made her feel queasy and thankful that she hadn't had any wine. A hangover would have made it far, far worse.

Miller had gone at crack of dawn, looking immaculate in his freshly ironed shirt and smelling enticingly of sandalwood aftershave, but leaving a trail of damp towels, used coffee mugs and toast crumbs in his wake. She wondered how his cleaner managed, or his wife, when he had had one.

Having stacked the dishwasher, switched it on and rinsed the takeaway cartons, the smell of spices still lingered, so she packed up the rubbish and recycling and took it all down to the bins. Returning to the main door she looked over at the net shops and thought about the first body, Simon, or Si, as Carl insisted he be called. She wondered how his wife was doing. Did his small child know he was gone for good? And the one yet to be born? How terrible never to meet your father. She wondered how they were all coping. It was always sad when someone died, but she couldn't help feeling that to lose your husband just when you needed his support most must be devastating.

Callie's thoughts turned to what Miller had said about who benefitted from the deaths. He was adamant that money had to be the root of the murders, but what if he was wrong? Carl had not shown any interest in the boat or the business since his brother and father had died. As far as she knew, he hadn't been out fishing since then, which was understandable. What if he had no desire to be a fisherman? Had anyone actually asked him if he wanted to be one? Or to own a boat? Had someone offered to buy it off him if he didn't want to be a fisherman himself? The only person she could think of who would know the answer to all or even any of her questions was Denny, so she walked across the road, through the dark, looming huts and the smaller sheds where they sold the fish that was not good enough for the market or their regular clients, and approached the area where the boats were beached when not out at sea.

Not surprisingly, a lot of boats were out and there were big empty spaces between piles of lobster pots, buoys and marker flags, but the RoseMarie was still there. Denny was busy cleaning the white plastic boxes they all used for the fish they caught, closely watched by a seagull who was making absolutely sure that no bits of fish had been left anywhere.

"Hiya," she said.

He looked up, confused for a moment until he recognised her.

"Morning," he said, then put the box he was holding down and straightened up. "What can I do for you, Doctor?"

"Oh, probably nothing. I just can't stop thinking about Simon… Si, and his family and everything that's happened. It's awful."

"That it is."

"Do you know how they are? If his wife is okay? And the baby?"

"As far as I know," he replied.

"And you've presumably not heard from Carl?"

"No, nothing from him at all, and not for want of trying. The police have been round asking too."

"I know, he seems to have disappeared." She looked at the boxes he had been cleaning. "Are you still going out fishing?"

"Sometimes. I can't handle the boat on my own and it's not often I can get anyone to crew. They were good at first, the lads, offering to help for the family's sake but…" He sighed. "If I don't go out, Shaz'll have no money coming in, so I do my best."

"That's good of you."

"Least I can do." He hesitated. "It's tough being a single mum."

He turned back to the boxes and seemed to think the conversation was over, but Callie had more questions.

"Were you there when that crew member got injured? Richard Simmons?"

"Surly Dick? Nah, it was before my time, but the way I heard it, it were his own fault. He was told time and time again to put the guard on the winch, but he never did. Stupid bugger."

"And Simon didn't tell him to do it?"

"Might've, might not. Wouldn't have made no difference."

"Was Carl there?"

"He was still at school then. Had a good excuse not to be out on the boat."

"Carl never wanted to be a fisherman, did he?"

"No, hated it." He shook his head and smiled. "Sea sick, really bad, never got over it, but his dad weren't having none of it."

As someone who was prone to seasickness herself, Callie could sympathise.

"What do you think he'll do with the RoseMarie?"

"Sell up, I s'pose."

"What about Sharon? I'm presuming she'll now own his share of the boat."

"Hadn't thought of that. Maybe she'll buy the lad out." Denny picked up a stack of boxes and started carrying them towards the net shops. Callie walked alongside him. "Don't suppose you know how much longer they'll be wanting to keep us out of the shed, do you?" he asked.

"Only I've lost half these boxes from having to leave them stacked outside already."

"Haven't they released it yet?"

"Tape's still on the door." Denny nodded to where she could see crime-scene tape still sealing the door to the shed.

"I'll check on that for you; they may just have forgotten to let you know."

She left him covering the boxes with a tarpaulin and walked between the tall sheds back towards the road and her home, glad to get away from the shadowy structures and the gloom they seemed to cast over everything.

Chapter 25

Callie had planned to go to the police station and ask when they would release the Porters' net shop so that Denny could use it again. As she parked her car and was walking to the entrance, she took a phone call from Mike Parton, who told her that they had decided on a simple coronial PM for Mrs Caldwell rather than a full forensic autopsy, because there were unlikely to be any charges relating to the death."

"I'm sorry?" she said. "No charges relating to her death?"

"Erm…" Parton cleared his throat. "It seems the CPS have looked at the case and felt that because the two perpetrators were not officially Mrs Caldwell's carers, they couldn't be charged with gross negligence manslaughter."

"Why ever not?"

"Because they didn't really have a duty of care, and the CPS don't think they have a reasonable chance of a guilty verdict for it, or for an unlawful and dangerous act manslaughter charge either, because the two of them could always argue that they had no idea that their actions would lead to her death."

"That's ridiculous," Callie almost shouted. Realising that she was being closely watched by the civilian at the front desk, she continued more quietly. "Of course their actions led to her death, and they must have known that they would."

"That's as maybe, but proving it beyond reasonable doubt would be difficult." Parton was, as usual, completely unflappable, but his lack of argument left her spoiling for a fight as she took the stairs to CID two at a time.

"Good afternoon, Dr Hughes, you will be pleased to know they found Carl and brought him in," Nigel told her with a smile.

"No, I will not be pleased to know that, Nigel." Callie was barely able to suppress her anger. "As I don't believe he had anything to do with his family's murders and you have probably put him in more danger by finding him and bringing him back here than if you had left him safely hidden."

"But…" was all Nigel managed to say before she continued.

"Is Steve in?" she was walking towards his office as she asked.

"Er, no, he's interviewing Carl with DS Jeffries at the moment."

Callie could see into Miller's office and it was empty. She rested her head against the door jam and counted to ten.

"What about the search for Mrs Caldwell's murderers, Nigel? Have they been found?"

Nigel looked startled.

"Murderers?"

"Mrs Caldwell died in hospital. Did Steve, DI Miller, I mean, not tell you? Between the dehydration and sepsis, she didn't stand a chance. Just because the CPS have chickened out on charging them with even manslaughter, I bet no one is even looking for the scumbags who did it, are they?"

"Oh, well, you see, we've been a bit…" Looking at Callie's face, Nigel changed what he was about to say. "Leave it with me, Dr Hughes, I'll get right onto it."

"And tell DI Miller that I want to speak to him as soon as he can spare me a moment, will you?"

Before Nigel could answer, Miller came into the room.

* * *

Callie was on her second glass of wine by the time Kate arrived at The Stag. One look at Callie and Kate went to the bar and ordered her another.

Placing the glass in front of her friend, along with a pint for herself and three packets of crisps, Kate asked, "Bad as that, is it?"

"Am I the only person who thinks that leaving an old lady lying in a filthy bed, starving her and not even giving her water, is a crime?"

"No, you're not." Kate took Callie's hand. "Of course it's a crime, it's just hard to prove it was done with the intent to kill."

"I know, but Steve basically said to forget about their treatment of Mrs Caldwell and concentrate on the fact that they will be done for drug dealing, when they find them, if they find them; oh, and maybe they'll be allowed to charge them with theft and trespass as well if they're lucky."

"He has a point, Callie. The CPS will know that any half-decent defence lawyer will say their clients were stupid, that they didn't mean her any harm but they just didn't know how to look after an old lady. Proving anything other than neglect would be impossible, after all, and they weren't really employed as carers officially, so they didn't have a duty of care or anything."

"Would you defend them that way? Knowing it wasn't true?"

"I don't know that it's not true and it's my job to defend people like them, even if I don't want to sometimes, Callie, you know that. I'd have to use every weapon at my disposal and, rest assured, they will still get sentenced for the drugs. If they've got records, it could be a substantial custodial sentence. Do you know if they found Class A drugs, or just Class Bs?"

"No As, just Bs and Cs, cannabis and benzodiazepines, but enough to charge them with intent to supply, if they ever find them."

"Oh." They both knew that the fact there were no class A drugs being dealt would significantly reduce any likely sentence the pair could expect. "But they took over someone else's flat to do it, and this will make the judge more inclined to make an example of them and go for a maximum custodial sentence. They could still get more for the drug dealing than for involuntary manslaughter. I don't think they'll be getting out any time soon, Callie, once they've found them, that is."

"Whatever they get, it's not enough, though, is it? Not for what they did." Callie took another large sip of wine. "The state they left her in is much, much worse than drug dealing. They should be done for murder." A tear slowly tracked down her cheek. "And I feel so guilty."

Kate kept quiet. She knew that nothing she'd say would make Callie feel any better, so she simply stroked her hand and let her talk.

"I had to tell Mr Herring she was dead and, you know what? He was the only one who actually seemed to understand." She sniffed and gratefully took the tissue Kate was holding out. "Although he was also more than a little relieved that his neighbours had gone." She blew her nose.

"I'll bet he was." Kate was glad to see Callie manage a small smile as she recalled Mr Herring's reaction to the news. "Here, have some crisps to soak up the alcohol," she said.

"I think you'll find that I probably need something more substantial than crisps for that," Callie replied, taking a handful.

"We can always have fish and chips on the way home," Kate said, "or a kebab."

Callie almost laughed and then grimaced again as a memory struck her.

"I shouted at Steve when I saw him."

"Hmm, well, it does seem a little unfair of you; after all, he's not the one to blame."

"But he is!" She paused. "Well, he is a little bit to blame. He's had all his team out looking for Carl and no one had even checked with forensics about the fingerprints and DNA found at Mrs Caldwell's. Soon as Nigel phoned the lab, they knew they were on the database and they had their names and last known addresses. They could have been out looking for them instead of wasting their limited resources and dragging Carl back."

"Okay, well, maybe he should have done more, but the CPS are the ones who decide on what charges are brought."

"You're right. I know that and I upset Steve and I should apologise."

"I'm sure he'll forgive you. He's probably forgotten it already; you know what men are like. The times I've apologised for something and they haven't got a clue why I'm apologising."

"I called him a useless wanker."

"Could have been worse."

"In front of his team."

"Ah, now that might have been a mistake."

"I know, but I was just so angry."

Kate patted her hand and looked at the empty wine glass.

"I think that calls for another round."

Chapter 26

Callie didn't hear from Miller that night despite several drunken texts she saw that she had sent him when she checked her phone the next morning. Some were conciliatory, some abusive and she had deleted them all, embarrassed that she had sent any of them. Hopefully Miller would do the same.

Making a promise to herself never to touch alcohol again, she drank a glass of water, took a couple of paracetamol and then, thankful that the morning was deemed to be an admin session to catch up on paperwork and training, she went back to bed.

When she next woke, she squinted at the clock and saw that it was gone ten o'clock and her mobile was ringing somewhere. Cursing at the fact that when she had checked her phone earlier she had left it in the living room, she got up.

Inevitably, the ringing had stopped by the time she got to it. She had a missed call from Steve Miller and he hadn't left a voicemail. Deciding that if she was going to call him back she would need tea, she went to the small kitchenette and filled the kettle. Her phone rang again before the kettle had boiled and this time, she did reach it in time to answer.

"Hi, Steve, sorry about last night." She wanted to get her apology out of the way as early as possible.

"Just wanted you to know we picked up your two drug dealers this morning."

It might have been her imagination but his voice seemed cold and almost formal.

"That is good news, thank you, and about—"

"I'll interview them once their legal representatives arrive," he cut in quickly, "but I imagine they will go 'no comment'."

No, he was definitely being deliberately formal.

"And what about Carl?" She mirrored his tone.

"He will be released later this morning."

"Good, I hope you haven't told him he needs to stay in Hastings because—"

She realised that she was talking to dead air. Miller had hung up on her. She felt like banging her head against the wall, she was so angry and frustrated, but that would only make her hangover worse.

Feeling a little restored after a cup of tea and a hot shower, Callie sat down with her laptop. Technically, she should catch up on her ongoing training with an update on prescribing, but instead she decided to put Mrs Caldwell out of her mind and concentrate her thoughts on who might have killed Jack, Simon and Marie Porter, as well as Rose Hudson, if, as she believed, it wasn't Carl.

She wrote a list of all the main contenders and crossed out the ones who were already dead. That left Carl, Surly Dick and Sharon Porter. After a moment's hesitation, she added 'unknown person', in acknowledgement of the fact that she didn't know everything about the family's life.

In a nod to Miller's theory that the killer would be someone who gained by their deaths, she drew an arrow from each of the dead people to whoever would benefit from it. She had to presume that everyone was intestate as she had no way of knowing what might be in anyone's will. Another place where her knowledge was incomplete.

The first victim, Simon Porter, had a fifty percent share of the RoseMarie and the fishing business. If he died intestate, that share would go to his wife, Sharon, so if someone was doing the murders for gain, she would be the number one suspect.

If Jack had died intestate, it was an interesting question as to whether Simon or Carl would inherit and one she would have to ask Kate about.

She knew that routine DNA samples would have been taken from both Simon and Jack's bodies to exclude them from the search for their killer's DNA. It would be interesting to map the family through all those DNA samples. Was Harry right in saying Simon was his son? If he was, then presumably Carl would inherit Jack's share. This was the fact that seemed to underpin Miller's campaign against Carl. And if Carl died, who would get his share? She would bet good money he hadn't made a will, so presumably Sharon's children would be the beneficiaries as his only surviving relatives. Was Sharon at risk because of this? Callie hoped she was well out of the way, because that would also mean her children were too, both the already born toddler and the soon to be born baby because, if anything happened to her, they would inherit the business in its entirety.

She didn't know who, if anyone, would get whatever money Rose had. Had she owned her own home? And if so, who would get it? Were there any living relatives? Or had she left everything to the church or the Cats Protection League?

Marie, judging by the meagre way she had lived, seemed to have nothing to leave anyone. She didn't even own her flat, it was rented.

Miller was right, the only people who seemed to gain anything from the deaths were Carl and Sharon. It was hard to imagine a heavily pregnant woman going round killing all these people; the sheer strength involved would make it unlikely but not beyond the realms of possibility.

She switched her thoughts to the theory that the motive was revenge for some past wrongdoing, a motive which seemed to fit the scenarios so much better than gain. Hanging someone used to be a punishment for murder, but the only murders she knew about were these ones.

She looked at the only remaining name on her list.

Surly Dick certainly had a grievance against Simon and Jack; he blamed them for the loss of his arm and not paying enough compensation, but why would he kill Rose and Marie?

There had to be someone else, she thought. She underlined the words 'unknown person' and then threw her pen down in disgust. There had to be a motive she was missing but she just didn't have enough information to know what it was. With Miller having blinkers on with regards to anyone other than Carl, there was little hope he would look elsewhere.

Callie tried to look at the training module she was supposed to be doing but couldn't settle. All these different scenarios were going through her head about who, and why, and how the murders had happened. To top it all she was still angry at how little regard was being given to the crime against her patient, however much she knew it was not the fault of the police.

There was just no way she could concentrate on drug interactions under the circumstances, so Callie decided that she couldn't sit still and wait for things to happen. She had to get out there and do something.

* * *

A call to the custody sergeant had revealed that Carl was being interviewed for a final time and would be released early afternoon. Next, Callie rang Mike Parton, the coroner's officer, and established that he was at the hospital mortuary, so she headed there first. It would give her the chance to speak to Matt Baxter as well, and tell them both why she wanted Mrs Caldwell to have a full post-mortem, so that every injury and indignity she had suffered at the hands of the drug dealers was thoroughly documented. When the two suspects went to court, she wanted there to be just cause for a longer sentence rather than a slap on the wrist for being low-level drug dealers.

What she hadn't bargained for was seeing Billy there.

"Hi, Callie," he said with a smile as she came out of the lift. Billy, Mike Parton and Matt Baxter were standing in the waiting area, probably because it was less claustrophobic than the pathologist's office.

"Hi," she replied. She could feel her nemesis – a blush – rising slowly up her neck. "What are you doing here?" she said lightly but there was no disguising her pleasure, tinged with anxiety, at seeing him.

"Just can't keep away from the place," Billy replied, then gestured at Parton. "I was just going over some of the salient points in the PMs for the coroner."

"And very helpful it was," Parton said. "Did you want to see me?"

"Um, yes, you and Matt, about Mrs Caldwell."

"Ah yes, the neglect case, very sad."

"But it wasn't just neglect, Mike." Callie couldn't keep the heat from her voice and she could feel all three men tense as she hurried on. "Her house was taken over by drug dealers who kept her in a room and refused anyone entry to check on her. They left her lying in her own waste, and didn't even give her water. They didn't just neglect her, they killed her."

Parton and Baxter exchanged embarrassed looks, which riled Callie even more.

"The coroner has ordered a coronial PM," Parton said. "Don't worry, Matt will do a thorough job."

Aware that she might have come across as a bit unbalanced, she consciously toned it down.

"I'm sure he will." She turned to the local pathologist and explained her concerns. "She had mild dementia, but she was perfectly capable of looking after herself, with a bit of support, before they arrived. I want – no, I need – to know what happened to change that. If nothing else, it might make a difference to the sentencing if there is a record of everything she went through."

"I understand, Callie. I'll check for anything abnormal, don't you worry." Matt patted her arm in a faintly condescending way and went back to his work. Parton made his excuses and left as well, leaving Callie and Billy alone.

"I've nothing urgent to get back to, so I can hang around for a while, make sure he takes blood to test for drugs and catalogues any untreated injuries, don't worry about that," he said.

"Won't Matt object to you watching over him?"

"I doubt it, he's a pretty laid-back bloke. Why has this case got to you like this?"

"Because I should have got to her earlier. Her neighbour had raised a concern and I phoned, sent letters and tried to visit, but didn't get hold of her, only her so-called carers, and I should have pushed more. I should have insisted the police visit, but they wouldn't agree to it until I had evidence they were dealing drugs from the flat, and it was too late by then."

"That's not your fault. You raised a welfare concern and they didn't act on it. That's down to them, not you."

"Which is what I told Steve."

"Ah, I'm not sure it's a detective inspector's job to do welfare checks."

"No, I know, but he could have pushed for a uniform to go round there."

"Yes, he could, but…" Billy paused, then said, "You look as though you need a hug." And put his arms around her.

She realised he was right and that this was what she had missed. She leant into the hug and snuggled against his shoulder. It felt good, comforting. No – more than that – it felt right. It seemed only natural for her to raise her face to him and for him to bend down and kiss her.

"Uh hmm," someone cleared their throat and Callie leapt back and turned to see Jim, the technician. "Dr Baxter is about to start an external examination on the old lady and wondered if you would care to join him, Dr Iqbal," he said, and couldn't resist a wink at Callie before turning and leaving.

"Told you so," Billy whispered, and hurried after Jim.

Chapter 27

Callie's next port of call was the police station, but instead of going in, she hung around outside the door that she knew Carl would be released from. It was a grey day, and the persistent mizzle left her reluctant to sit on the damp grass. She could feel her hair frizzing.

She had a takeaway coffee and a pain-au-chocolat, her go-to comfort food, which she was eating under the shelter of a large horse chestnut tree. She had had her pastry and almost finished her coffee when she saw the door open and Carl and his legal adviser emerge. She waited for him to say goodbye to his brief, who clapped him on the shoulder and hurried towards the car park. Callie's heart went out to the young lad who looked completely lost as she walked towards him.

"Hello, Carl," she said, dropping her pastry bag and the nearly finished coffee into a bin. "I spoke to you after your brother died, do you remember?"

He nodded in response.

"Can I talk to you for a minute?" Seeing him hesitate, she added, "By the way, I don't think you are responsible for any of this."

He still didn't look sure.

"Maybe I can buy you lunch?"

Callie wasn't surprised that it was her offer of lunch that finally swayed him, because she knew that the food options available in the police station wouldn't satisfy the average teenage boy. He followed her to a nearby café with a reputation for its enormous portions, and for serving chips with pretty much everything. Callie didn't mention that it was also known for the number of policemen who frequented it because of its proximity to the station. She crossed her fingers no one she knew would be in there, particularly Bob Jeffries. Or Steve Miller.

As she tentatively pushed open the door, she saw she was in luck and hurriedly led Carl to a table in the far corner before going to order the all-day breakfast for him and two cups of coffee.

"So, why don't you think I killed all my family?" he asked as she set his coffee down in front of him and sat down.

"Because I can't think of any reason why you might do that."

"The police seem to think I did it for a share in the sodding boat. Idiots. I hate the bloody thing. I'll give it to Sharon as soon as the lawyers say I can, but they say it's months away. I have to go to some kind of court."

"Probate court."

"Yeah. Don't see why I can't just tell them to stuff it and give everything away."

Callie knew it would be a long while before probate was granted.

"You don't want to be a fisherman then?"

"No fucking way." He paused as his food was put down in front of him, shining and slimy with grease. He grabbed the smiley-face tomato ketchup dispenser and squeezed a dollop onto his plate. "I want to go to art college," he told her, looking at her from under his fringe, clearly expecting a negative reaction. "I've got a place, in Brighton. Dad thought I was joking, called me a pansy, but it's what I want to do."

"Then that's what you should do," she said.

He seemed so young, far too young to be worrying about all this. He was eighteen, for goodness' sake, and deserved some carefree years in college.

"Carl, I need to ask you about the past, about anyone who might bear a grudge against your family. Do you know of anyone who might?"

He thought for a while as he ate.

"Not really," he said, but she noticed that he couldn't quite look her in the eye.

"Come on, Carl, it's important."

"Well, there's this guy called Richard, 'Surly Dick' as we all call him. He was in an accident on board and wasn't happy with the compensation he got."

"We know about him, but he has an alibi for at least some of the murders."

"He could have paid someone to do it."

"Yes, and the police are looking into it."

"When they're not trying to pin it on me?"

He had a point.

"I'll make sure they look into it properly, that's a promise," she said, crossing her fingers under the table. She didn't think Steve or Bob Jeffries would be happy to hear from her any time soon. "Anyone else?"

He hesitated, concentrating on his food for a while.

"Look, I know that Simon well – that Harry Hudson was his father. That must have caused a rift. Come on, Carl, tell me if anyone had a reason to be angry – your life might just depend on it."

He finally looked at her and pushed the unfinished food away. After a few moments of soul-searching, he gave a small sigh. He had reached a decision.

"Just after Uncle Harry died, this woman came out of the woodwork. Said Harry was the father of her son. She tried to make a claim against the will. Wanted Uncle Harry's share of the boat to go to her son, not Si, but they did DNA tests and he wasn't related to Harry, so he got nothing."

This was news to Callie. This was clearly someone who could have felt wronged by the family.

"Do you know who he was?"

Carl shook his head.

"I was only fifteen or maybe just sixteen at the time, and they didn't tell me much, most of that I got from listening to the grown-ups talking." He was looking shamefaced, guilty almost, and Callie wondered if there was more he wasn't telling her.

"And he hasn't been back in touch?"

"Not as far as I know." He seemed genuinely at a loss. "Look, you won't tell the police about going to college, will you?" he said as he finished his coffee. "Only they'd think I killed everyone to get enough money to get away from here, but I was planning on just walking out. I'm an adult, so they couldn't stop me, could they?" He didn't seem too sure.

"No, they couldn't stop you," she said hesitantly, before adding, "but don't do anything rash. After all, selling your share of the boat could help pay your way through college."

"Sharon hasn't got any money and I wouldn't want to sell it to someone outside the family." He looked out of the window, suddenly blinking back tears, then continued in a husky voice that made her want to give him a hug. "It's a family business, Sharon and the sprogs are the only family I've got left."

* * *

Callie looked at her watch as she waited for Kate to finish her phone call. She was due for a session in the GP-led unit at the hospital from six o'clock, when the surgeries began to close, and she was cutting it fine. The out-of-hours GP unit was where patients who called 111 were sent when they were not considered urgent enough for A&E.

Finally, Kate was winding things up with her client and saying goodbye. She put down the phone with a sigh and held a hand up to stop Callie.

"Just let me make a note of what I need to do," she said, rapidly scribbling on a legal pad. "There, that's done, now what can I help you with? And can it wait until we get to the pub?"

"Sorry. I'm in out-of-hours care this evening, so…" She looked at her watch again.

"Fair enough. Fire away."

"Apparently there was a challenge to Harry Hudson's will, an unsuccessful one, from a person who thought her son was another of Harry's illegitimate offspring."

"Ooh, why was it unsuccessful?" Kate was almost rubbing her hands together in excitement.

"DNA tests showed that the boy wasn't related to Harry."

"Who did they compare him with?"

"Well, his mother and Simon, I think, but I don't really know. It would make sense that they did that. It would tell them whether or not he had any of Harry's DNA, given that Harry had been cremated by then."

"They can get DNA from ashes now, can't they?"

"Not really," Callie answered her. "It's theoretically possible if bits of bones or teeth remain but unlikely to be successful as the heat will probably have broken the DNA down."

"Okay, and he's probably had his ashes scattered by now, so we can't do a retest. So, let's make a list of what we need to know."

"First thing is who it was, both the person making the claim and their mother, I suppose."

"You're thinking that this person may feel cheated in some way?"

"Well, yes, Harry wasn't a rich man, but he had the half a boat and a pretty good life. Perhaps they wanted to be part of it. Also, if they've been brought up thinking they were Harry's son and they find out they are not… I mean, has their mum been lying to them all this time? And who is their real father? It could really mess with their head."

"I can imagine. Do you know that it was a boy, this supposed Hudson child?"

"Carl referred to him as a bloke, but he was only a boy when it happened so he might not have it right."

Kate pulled over her legal pad and selected a fresh page.

"Right, well, we know when Harry died." She looked up. "Do you know which solicitors handled probate?"

"It was a will-writing service," Callie said. "I know you don't approve but lots of people use them because they are cheaper than using a solicitor."

Kate grunted in response.

"But if they wanted a DNA test to refute a claim against the will, they would probably get legal advice," she added. At least she hoped they would.

"And Carl doesn't know who they used?"

"No, and it's not like there's anybody he can ask now, is there?"

"Fair point well made." Kate carried on writing on the pad. "Okay, leave it with me and get on with your doctoring. I'll call round and see if I can find out who handled it."

"Will they tell you? I mean, isn't it confidential?"

"They will tell me if I suggest there might be an ongoing case for them, with money attached. You'd be amazed at what information the hope of a nice fat fee gets you."

Actually, Callie wouldn't be amazed, or even faintly surprised. And nor was she surprised that Kate hadn't finished her probing.

"Heard from Steve yet?"

"No, not really, just to let me know they were letting Carl go."

Kate gave her a hard look.

"He's not responded to your numerous messages and voicemails apologising then?"

"No." Callie squirmed in her seat; Kate knew her too well.

"And?" Kate asked.

"Billy was at the mortuary."

"And?"

"He gave me a hug because I was upset and we, well, we sort of kissed."

"Sort of?"

"Well, okay, we kissed, and Jim, the mortuary technician saw."

"And how do you feel about the kiss? Was it nice?"

"Well, yes and no."

"Tell me more."

"Well, it felt completely natural and nice at the time, but now, well, I can't help feeling like I cheated on Steve."

Kate put her head in her hands. "It was a kiss, not full-on sex on one of the body trolleys or standing up in the laundry cupboard, for goodness' sake," she said.

"I know, but still…"

"Go on, get off to your doctoring and stop being such a wazzock."

Callie smiled; a dose of Kate was exactly what she needed when she knew she was overthinking things but couldn't stop herself.

"And stop calling Steve. Let him sulk for a while and realise what he's missing," Kate called out as Callie left and hurried back to the hospital and the out-of-hours GP unit.

* * *

Thank you, Mr Plod the policeman, for finding the boy for me. Of course, they don't know they did me a favour, but they did, all the same. He's back home, living at his father's old place. I wonder how long before the landlord boots him out for non-payment of rent? He doesn't know it yet, but he doesn't have to worry about that. He will be dead long before he can be evicted.

He is being careful; I'll give him that. He's not as stupid as he looks. He has mates round all the time and never ventures out alone, but I can be patient. I can stalk my prey and he will be alone one day and then I'll get him, the last one who cheated me. He was only young then, but he's grown up now and he still hasn't spoken up about what he did, what they all did. They will be punished. Every last one of them.

Chapter 28

The first thing Callie did when she woke up the next morning was to check her phone in case she had missed a call or message from Steve. But she hadn't. No calls, no messages, just a cold, hard silence. He was clearly much better at sulking than she had realised, or maybe she had misjudged things so badly that she had really upset him. Either way, there was nothing she could do until he was talking to her again.

The evening she had spent working in the GP-led unit had meant that she was kept busy with a steady stream of patients needing antibiotics, reassurance, to be sent on to A&E or referred back to their own doctor in the morning, so she had found it relatively easy to heed Kate's advice. She had not contacted Miller, not even with a cheeky text message. It had been much harder to resist the temptation once she got home. She had put her phone in her bedside drawer, gone for a long soak in the bath and then to bed without checking it again. She had told herself that if he had sent a message, it would do him good to wait for a reply. Kate would be proud of her, she thought, but, unsurprisingly, she hadn't slept well.

At five o'clock she finally gave up, got up and took a cup of tea out to the balcony along with her laptop and phone. She kept asking herself how had she managed in her last flat without any outside space. She would never again live anywhere without a balcony or a courtyard garden at the very least. She shivered in the cold morning air and wrapped her dressing gown more tightly around her. Still no messages, so she booted up her laptop, checked the news and found nothing to cheer herself up.

Happy that she could leave the task of identifying the lawyers involved in the original will dispute to Kate, Callie looked at the hundreds of unread emails in her inbox, singling out the few interesting ones and deleting the rest.

Matt Baxter had let her know that Mrs Caldwell's autopsy did not throw up anything unexpected. He also reassured her that tissue and blood samples had been sent off and marked urgent, so the initial results should be back within the week. Some would be back faster than others. There was a separate email from Billy which re-iterated these facts; she couldn't help noticing that he had signed off with a couple of 'x's and she smiled. Miller had never done that; in fact Miller didn't really do email, WhatsApp or any kind of social media. He also didn't seem to do phone calls or text messages when he was angry and sulking. Knowing that there was nothing she could do to speed up the pathology results, or her boyfriend, she sent quick responses saying thank you to both pathologists, hesitating before adding a couple of 'x's to Billy's, erasing them, then putting them back in and pressing send before she could change her mind again.

That done, Callie went back inside and spent the morning catching up on all the work associated with her day job. She did a three-hour telephone clinic and asked ten people to come in and see her for further assessment during the afternoon.

It wasn't until later that evening, once again on the balcony with a cup of tea and listening to the noises of the town around her, that she finally got an interesting call.

"Just walking over to you, if you're home," Kate said.

"Yup, just sitting on the balcony having a cup of tea."

"I'll be with you in five minutes and, let me tell you, I have some good news."

Checking her cupboards quickly, Callie realised that she still hadn't been out and bought wine, or food for that matter, but she did have some bottles of the beer that Kate liked and Miller didn't, so that would have to do. Callie was happy to stick to tea.

Kate said she was too cold for the balcony, so they sat down inside and Callie waited patiently for Kate to settle herself and drink some of her beer. Opening her briefcase, Kate took out her pad and a bag of crisps to share.

"Because you never have any snacks in the house."

"Because I'd eat them," Callie explained.

"Well, duh, that's what they're for."

"Come on, don't keep me waiting. What's this good news?" Callie had reached the end of her patience.

"I found the solicitor who handled the Hudson end of the will dispute."

"And?"

"He sent me the case file."

"That's good."

"You were right, a woman came forward claiming that her son's father was Harry Hudson and that, as her child was his oldest son, he should inherit the half-share of the boat, not Simon. You'll remember that Harry's will left his share to his *only* son, so there would certainly have been grounds to challenge it, especially if she could prove Harry knew he had a child."

"What happened to her claim?"

"They arranged DNA tests to make sure the lad really was another illegitimate child of Harry's"

"And?"

Kate had a twinkle in her eye that told Callie there was something really interesting that she had found in those files, but Kate was going to keep her waiting as she took another swig of beer and grabbed a handful of crisps.

"So," Kate finally started, "In order to prove or disprove that Harry was this lad's father. DNA was needed from both sons."

"Of course. Both boys' DNA would be a mix of their mother's and Harry's and there should be enough similarity between them to show they are half-brothers."

"That's right. Now, if I were going to do DNA tests to prove or disprove a paternity case like this, I would want proof the person I was taking the swab from, *was* the person it was supposed to be and I would want the actual swabbing to be witnessed by me, and I would want to have the swab in my sight from the beginning of the procedure to sending them off."

"Like chain of custody for police samples?"

"Exactly. Because only then could I attest that the sample was absolutely and unequivocally taken from the person as stated."

"But that's not what happened?" Callie could feel a tingle. This was it, this was the clue that would solve the murders, she just knew it.

"No. Don't get me wrong, the solicitor signed a statement saying that he can attest that the sample came from the named donor, Simon Porter, but checking the files, Marie Porter came in with her son to have the sample taken, and both mother and son signed statements to say that the boy being swabbed was Simon Porter. But," she paused for dramatic effect, "how do we know it was? There doesn't seem to have been any sort of check that the boy was actually Simon other than them saying it was."

"You think it might have been a random boy?" Callie couldn't quite believe that.

"Possibly, but wasn't it more likely to be the other son? The one who *didn't* have Harry for a father? There's only a few years between them, isn't there?"

"Five years," Callie was deep in thought. Surely the solicitor would have noticed that he was younger than Simon was supposed to be? Carl was tall and quite mature looking, but when he was fifteen? Could he have posed as a twenty-year-old?

"Do you honestly think they could have got away with it?" Callie asked.

"Well, this solicitor definitely cut corners and didn't exactly comply with best practice, or even minimum standards, if you ask me. And I won't be recommending him anytime soon, that's for sure."

"But if the claimant's solicitor had known how slack the process had been, they would have contested it, wouldn't they?"

"But how could they know? They had the solicitor's signed statement that the swab came from Simon Porter, so they just accepted it."

"Do you think he was in on it? The solicitor, I mean."

"Possibly, but my money's on him just being incompetent."

"And I'm guessing there was no familial similarity found between the two samples?" Callie asked.

"No, none at all."

Suddenly, Carl's reticence to speak up made sense. He knew he had been used to make sure the claim was thrown out.

Callie jumped up. "What's the claimant's name? I have to go to Steve with this."

"Doesn't say on here, he is just referred to by as 'the claimant' but it does give the name of the legal practice representing him, so I'll try and get hold of them today."

"It's a local firm, is it?"

"No, they're based in Rye. And they might not be keen on talking to me."

"We have to find out his name. He has a real reason to have a grudge and to blame the whole family. They all must have been complicit in the swab switch. Jack, Marie, Simon and Carl." She stopped. "But wait! What about Rose Hudson? Why did he kill her?"

Kate gave Callie a slightly smug smile. "She made a statement saying that she knew nothing of this person who was making a claim and that Harry could not have met her, let alone fathered a child with her, because he wouldn't mix with her sort of woman. In the notes, she apparently told the solicitor that the woman was widely known to be a local prostitute and anyone could have been the father of her child."

"Ouch! She absolutely crushed that poor woman. Why would she do that?"

"I have an idea about that," Kate said and fished out a printed copy of Harry Hudson's will. "If you go back to the will, here" – she pointed to a paragraph – "Harry left his share of the business to Simon."

"Which was the fifty percent share of the boat."

"Yes, but the house he and Rose lived in was also owned by the company at the time. When Harry died, it should have been sold to give Simon and Jack their half shares, but it wasn't, and Rose seems to have stayed living there until she died."

Callie sat back, as she took this news in. "They paid her off," she said. "Told her she could stay in the house if she helped them put the claim to bed."

"More than that," Kate continued. "According to the records, the full ownership of the house was transferred to her soon after she made that statement."

"That seems a high price to pay for what was essentially just a supporting statement. I mean, full ownership of the house?"

"But maybe it wasn't just that she made a supporting statement. If she knew that this claimant really was Harry's son, she would have to have known they'd switched the son taking the test. The house was payment for her not snitching on them," Kate said.

This made sense to Callie. "Probate won't have been granted on Rose's will yet, so we can't know for sure, but I bet she leaves the house wholly to Simon as part of that agreement."

"Or to Jack and Simon jointly. Either way, that means the house will go to Simon's wife."

Callie stood up. "Right, I have to go and tell Steve all this. We have to trace that claimant. Steve can demand the solicitors tell him, can't he?"

"Client confidentiality," Kate reminded her as she also stood and grabbed her coat. "He'd need a warrant. But I'll try and persuade someone to talk to me. I might go back to my original source and see if he ever knew who it was. Might just be gossip but–"

"That's better than nothing," said Callie. As she hurried round finding her bag, coat and keys, she added, "And thanks, Kate. You've come up trumps again."

"If I find out who the guy is, you will owe me dinner."

"Agreed."

"Are you going to ring Miller and warn him you're coming round?"

"Not a chance," Callie told her. "He's not answering his phone anyway so I'll have to do this face to face."

"Just don't call him a useless wanker again."

Callie closed the door behind them as they left.

"I'm not making any promises," she said, half under her breath.

Chapter 29

The incident room still had a smattering of people present, mainly civilians taking phone calls or adding information onto the database, but a lot of the detectives had left for the night. The light was on in Miller's corner office and she could see him at his desk, talking to someone by the filing cabinets. As she strode to the door, she realised the other person was, inevitably, Bob Jeffries. Miller looked up and frowned as she approached his office door. He wasn't going to give her a friendly welcome, that was for sure.

"Do you have a minute?" she asked, simultaneously removing the junk from the visitor's chair and sitting down.

"Give us a moment, would you, Bob?" Miller asked his sergeant.

"Sure you don't want me to referee?" Jeffries said, but obediently went to the door.

"Bob is welcome to stay and hear about the person who has killed most of the Hudson and Porter families, and – breaking news – it's not Carl." Callie was still holding the files she had removed from the chair and, looking round in vain for somewhere to put them within easy reach, handed them to Jeffries instead.

He plonked them on top of the filing cabinet and then leant against it expectantly, a small smile on his lips.

"Go on, then, who is it?" Jeffries asked.

Callie turned back to Miller, who was still frowning but raised an eyebrow inviting her to enlighten them.

"A bit of history first," she said, "because you were right, Steve, this is about who gains, or rather about who *should* have gained from these deaths. But I was right too, because it is also about revenge. No, don't interrupt." She could see he had been about to. "It all goes back to Harry Hudson's will, where he left his share of the boat and the house he lived in, which was owned by the firm for tax reasons or something, I think, to his only son, Simon Porter."

"We know that." Miller finally managed to interrupt.

"But did you know that the will was contested by a person who said he was also Harry's son, and older to boot?"

Miller sat back in his chair. This was clearly news to him and she tried to hide a small triumphant smile, unsuccessfully.

"Go on, what happened next?" he finally said.

"There were DNA tests and some evidence to suggest that the Porter family colluded in substituting Carl's DNA for Simon's, with the inevitable result that this lad came back as not a match, because Carl's father was, as you know, Jack not Harry."

"How did they pull that one off?" Jeffries asked.

"Sloppy procedures by the firm of solicitors handling the Porter family DNA collection."

"In what way?" Miller asked her. "Doesn't there have to be some sort of chain of evidence, or something?"

"You would think so, wouldn't you? But the solicitor didn't really check the lad being swabbed was Simon Porter, they just told him it was." Callie wasn't quite ready to tell them that it was actually likely to have been Carl.

"Bloody hell!"

"Who was this other claimant?" Miller asked.

"Kate's trying to find out through the law firm used to make the claim, but they may not agree to name names, under the circumstances, so you will have to get a warrant. Also, the original samples will have been destroyed by now, although the test results should still be available from the solicitor's records, I would hope. All you need to do to prove my theory is correct is compare the sample they said was Simon's to the ones you have already taken for him and Carl."

"Right, Bob, get someone onto the lab."

Jeffries hurried out of the office.

Miller picked up the phone and turned to Callie, "What's this solicitor's name? The one for the Porter family."

She handed him the sheet of paper Kate had written it down on.

"They'll be closed at this time of night," she said.

"I'm getting a warrant ready for the morning." He started punching numbers into the phone.

Callie stilled his hand with a touch. "Before you do that, what's happening with Mrs Caldwell's killers?"

"They'll be charged with dealing Class Bs and Cs and possibly theft, obtaining money and goods fraudulently, and any other charges the CPS authorise. I know you are angry it's not more, but there really is nothing more I can do for her, Callie."

"You could press the CPS to make the case for manslaughter."

"They won't do that and they are right not to. There is no point in trying to fight losing battles, it just wastes court time and public money."

"Of course you could do more," Callie said. Despite her resolve to stay cool, she couldn't stop herself. "You are the SIO, you could tell them to look again, or ask for someone more senior to make the decision. Show them you are fighting for your victim," she told him, wagging a finger as she spoke and realising that her voice had risen, not just in tone but in decibels, and that a flush was making its way up her neck to her cheeks.

Miller looked out of his office window and she thought he was checking to see if anyone had noticed their argument. They probably had. Bob Jeffries certainly wouldn't have missed it, even if he was on the phone to the lab.

"Grow up," Miller hissed at her. "This is the real world and sometimes people don't get the justice they deserve."

"Maybe that's because they don't get the police they deserve," she told him as she stood up, cheeks flaming. "Maybe you shouldn't need me to come in and tell you what you are doing wrong and what you should be investigating time after time."

She walked out of his office, head held high and looking straight ahead, making sure she didn't catch anyone's eye as she left.

* * *

Callie sat on the sofa, head in her hands, hardly able to speak. Not because she was upset, but because she was still angry.

Kate had sat her down and poured her a glass of wine as soon as she stepped over the threshold, but Callie hadn't taken so much as a sip.

"I've really done it now," she finally managed to say.

"I'm sure it's not as bad as you think it is." Kate rubbed her back in what she hoped was a sympathetic and reassuring manner. "Was Steve not prepared to listen?"

"Steve and I…" Callie stopped to let out what sounded like a mix of a groan and a sob. "Well, I think it's fair to say we are over. He might say he likes strong women who aren't afraid to voice their opinions, but I think I probably took it a bit too far."

"You called him a useless wanker again, then?"

"Pretty much." Callie sniffed and Kate handed her a tissue. "It's not just us finished as a couple – I could cope with that – but I'm not sure I can ever work with him again."

"He'll get over it."

"No, no, I don't think he will, and Bob Jeffries certainly won't. It's going to be too awkward." She hiccupped. "And it's not as if it did any good. Those two drug dealers will get away with killing Mrs Caldwell and I'm not even sure I've convinced him that Carl didn't kill everyone."

"Are they at least looking into this claimant?"

"I think so. Steve was getting a warrant for the solicitors as I left."

"Well, that's good at least. Can you imagine how he must have felt having always thought that Harry was his father and then suddenly finding out he wasn't."

"Yes and he lost the boat as well as his father." Callie could imagine how wronged he must have felt.

"Exactly. I wonder if he ever worked it out."

"Worked what out?"

"That they'd pulled a fast one and he really was Harry's son."

"I can see that being a pretty good motive." For revenge, for punishment, it all seemed to fit. Much better than simply killing the family off for ownership of the business.

"Another thought did occur to me," Kate said. "Has anyone actually looked at Sharon? I mean, she does stand to gain as much as Carl from these deaths, and not just a boat as we now know but quite possibly a house too."

"I know, but she also loses the most. Her husband, the father of her children."

"That hasn't stopped some women. Has anyone checked the state of her relationship with her husband? Were they happy?"

"Denny, the crewman on the RoseMarie, said they were and she certainly seemed pretty upset when I saw her." Callie blew her nose. She seemed to be over her crying fit.

"Okay, not definitive proof but pretty good for starters." Kate topped up her own wine glass.

Callie had yet to start on hers.

"Would you rather have a cup of tea?" Kate asked.

"No, no." Callie smiled. "I just needed to get that out. Why are men such, such…"

"Useless wankers?"

"Yes." Callie laughed.

"Well, they're not all like that," Kate told her firmly. "Look at Sam, he's lovely."

"Yes, yes he is."

Sam was Kate's current boyfriend, and the most serious she had ever known Kate to have. He had certainly lasted a lot longer than any of her previous ones.

"He's asked me to move in with him." Kate suddenly confided and looked at her friend anxiously.

"That's wonderful!" Callie said and hugged Kate. "Will he be able to work from here?"

"No, no, he's asked me to move up to London."

There was a moment's silence as Callie took in the implications of this revelation.

"Will you be commuting from London then?"

Kate sighed.

"You know I've been thinking for some time that I can't continue as a one-man band."

"I thought that meant you were thinking of taking on a partner, or an assistant."

"It's not that easy to find someone who fits the bill, and I can't stay as I am. I have to do absolutely everything, which means I have to turn down a lot of work, unless I want to work twenty-four hours a day, which I don't. On top of that, I have to pay all the costs of running the business as well. It's just not economical."

"But if you work in someone else's firm, you won't be as free to make your own choices. You always said that was what you liked about working for yourself."

"I know, but a position has come up at the GMC and I will be fairly autonomous."

"You'll be working with Sam?"

"Not directly, no; we'll be in different areas."

There was a pause as Callie thought about this.

"Are you sure about this? I mean, you haven't known him long."

"I've known him long enough and yes, I am sure. I've been meaning to tell you for ages, but I needed to think it all through and make my mind up."

"I understand, honestly, but please tell me you're not doing this just because you're fed up with work."

"I'm not. Although, there's a lot to be said for a steady income."

Callie blew her nose again and drank some of her wine as she took all this in.

"I know it makes sense, and Sam is lovely. I'm just being selfish wanting you to stay here."

"You could say the same about me, being selfish for wanting to leave."

They hugged and Callie sniffed again. Kate handed her the tissues and then took one for herself.

"What about this place?" Callie indicated the house around her; she had always felt so happy here when she visited. The cottage was so homely. With its bright colours, comfy chairs and mismatched cushions, it reflected Kate's larger-than-life personality.

"We'll keep it as a weekend cottage, a holiday home, so don't worry, you're not getting rid of me. I'll still be here, almost as often as I am now, and London really isn't that far if you fancy a few days away."

No matter how Kate reassured her, Callie knew that her life was about to change without Kate just a short walk away whenever she needed a friend – which was pretty often, it seemed.

Chapter 30

Callie found it hard to concentrate on her work the next morning. She was in the surgery, triaging the early morning requests for a call back, but she kept having to go back over the list because she was sure she was allocating patients to the wrong member of the team. She finally had them all sorted and was working her way through the patients she had left for herself to call back, when her mobile rang.

"Hi," she said, unable to keep the smile from her voice.

"I know you must be busy," Billy said. "I won't take long but Matt Baxter rang me with some news."

"Oh, yes?" She sat up straighter in her chair, all business now.

"He's calling Steve Miller and the coroner's officer, but he thought you might like to know that the tox results are back on Mrs Caldwell and there were high levels of temazepam and its metabolites."

"More than a clinical dose?"

"Yes, though that might of course be explained if her liver or kidney function was poor. The question you will be asked is if she was prescribed temazepam at any point, or if this comes from her flatmates."

Callie clicked through to Mrs Caldwell's clinical notes.

"No, she has never been prescribed it." Callie took a deep breath. "Those bastards were drugging her to keep her quiet. This changes everything."

"It does indeed," Billy agreed. "It means the CPS will almost certainly have to agree to a charge of manslaughter now. Not gross negligence but because of an unlawful act."

They both knew that those were the two criteria for a charge of manslaughter. Personally, Callie thought it ought to actually push the charge up to murder, but she also knew that they would plead not guilty and say that they didn't know the dose would kill her. Manslaughter would have to do.

* * *

Predictably, Miller didn't call to let Callie know that the two drug dealers had been re-arrested and charged with manslaughter, but Jayne did.

"It's still not a slam-dunk but they think there's a reasonably good chance that they'll be found guilty. If they actually turn up to court, that is."

"They didn't get remanded then?"

"Nope, no chance of that, not for something like this."

"And you think they'll just disappear?"

"I would, if I were them. Wouldn't you? Neither of them seems to have any ties to the area, apart from through dealing, and they can deal drugs pretty much anywhere, just need to hook up with a gang somewhere else. I mean, why risk going to prison for a few years, when you can just up sticks, call yourself something else and start all over again in a new area?"

Callie knew it was the likely outcome. Low-level drug dealers need never be out of a job, provided they were prepared to work with the local gangs and didn't tread on anyone else's toes.

"I feel better knowing that even if they do that, there will be warrants out on them. Their fingerprints are in the system and they are sure to be picked up again in the future, when they do something stupid again."

"Yes, and the chances of them being remanded then will be significantly improved if they've failed to attend a court appearance here," Jayne said.

Callie found it depressing knowing that all too often, in the short term at least, criminals could get away with what was, to Callie, murder, but she knew it was the simply the way things were.

"What about the other murders? What about Carl? Have you been able to identify the will claimant yet?" she asked.

There were a few moments of silence.

"I'm not really supposed to talk to you about that," Jayne said. "Orders from above, if you know what I mean."

"No, no, of course, I understand," Callie said through gritted teeth. Miller wasn't going to forgive her for that outburst so easily, it seemed. If at all.

"Your information has been followed up, though," Jayne told her. "I don't want you to think we've ignored it, it's just that, well, it doesn't seem to go anywhere because the bloke's dead."

"Dead?"

"Fishing accident a year ago," Jayne informed her. "So, it can't be him killing everyone off."

To say Callie was disappointed at the news was an understatement.

* * *

"I'd pinned all my hopes on the claimant being the killer, it just fitted, you know?" Callie told Kate.

"Yeah, I'd sort of assumed we were on the right track. It's looking more and more like it has to be Carl then, doesn't it?"

They were sitting in the café by Kate's office as she was busy with the first stages of winding up her firm in readiness for her move to London and more regular employment.

"I can't believe that; his motive just doesn't hold together. He doesn't even want to keep the boat." Callie paused to move her food around her plate. Somehow, the state of her love life, the thought of Kate moving away and the setbacks with the murder investigation meant that she had lost her appetite. "Do you think it could be someone associated with the claimant, you know, taking revenge for him even though he's dead?"

Kate was busy eating her own lunch of a loaded panino, but that didn't stop her eyeing up Callie's unfinished sandwich and crisps.

"That actually sounds like a good idea. His grieving partner, or a child perhaps?"

"I don't think any child of his would be old enough to do all these killings, but I like the grieving partner angle. Do you think we could find out more about him? Will his details be confidential still, even though he's dead?"

Having finished her sandwich, Kate wiped her mouth with a napkin.

"Officially yes, but I might be able to find out his name from the firm, by using all my very persuasive charm or rather by offering them some of my regular clients in return. Then we can look for anyone connected," Kate said. "Are you eating those crisps? Clearing out my filing cabinets is hard work, a better workout than the gym."

"As if you'd know. When did you last go to the gym to exercise?" Callie shoved her plate away. "I'm done. You can have them, and the sandwich, if you want."

"Ugh, tuna salad? You must be joking. Way too healthy for me."

"It would be good to know how he died, this claimant chap, as well. He must have been quite young. I can't help wondering, what if he was the first one to be killed? The first victim?"

"Gosh…" Kate paused with a crisp halfway to her mouth. "I hadn't thought of that. I'll get on it right away. Much more interesting than shredding old files."

Chapter 31

Callie was sitting in Kate's office amid a sea of half-packed boxes.

"What are you going to do with all this stuff?" she asked.

"I have it all worked out, don't you worry," Kate said as she brought two mugs of tea through from the tiny kitchenette. "That pile of boxes will be going to Stokely, Harding and Smith. That pile is going in my attic, and that pile" – she indicated the largest one with her elbow and tried not to spill any of the tea – "is being shredded and ditched. I've had to pay a company to do it because my shredder took one look at how much there was and promptly died. They collect it all tomorrow, thank goodness, and the new leaseholders want all the office furniture, so that will be that."

"That's good." Callie smiled but inside she was feeling suddenly alone.

"Now, let's look at the displacement activity I have been indulging in rather than pack." Kate clicked on her laptop and, after a few keystrokes, turned it round to show Callie.

"Stokely, Harding and Smith were the firm that handled the claimant's case and they told me his name after I bribed them with my current caseload. They won't be so happy when they go through the paperwork, believe me – a right bunch of losers, the lot of them. Now, this is what came up when I googled his name."

Callie took the laptop and saw that the page was showing a newspaper report of a fishing tragedy.

"Leisure boat 'The Seamaid' sinks off Dover with loss of one man," the headline screamed, and Callie went on to read about a small boat that got into difficulties and sank in bad weather a year earlier.

"I don't remember reading about this."

"It wasn't in the local papers here and it didn't rate any national coverage. The man who died was David Howe, from Hastings, aged twenty."

"And he was the man who claimed he was Harry Hudson's eldest son?"

"That's right, his body was never found. The survivor, Dennis Brown, was a bit older and the more experienced sailor. Questions were asked at the inquest about what they were doing out there anyway, as neither of them were from Dover. Apparently, they were just visiting on a fishing trip. They'd hired the boat for the day and the weather was calm. Dennis Brown stated that there was a sudden squall and the boat capsized."

The newspaper article continued with pictures of the lifeboat bringing a sailor back with them.

"Hang on a tick." Callie looked at the picture and then zoomed in. Kate looked over her shoulder.

"He looks young, doesn't he?" Kate said. "For a thirty-year old."

Callie continued to examine the picture, zooming in and out. She needed to make the picture bigger to see, but it got too blurry to make out the surviving sailor's features when she made it too large.

"Was there any coverage of the inquest?"

"Kate leant over and clicked through to another article which showed a man leaving the court, with his hand up to cover his face as the photograph was taken.

She flicked between that photo and the one of him after the rescue.

Finally, she sat back.

"What is it? Do you recognise him?" Kate asked.

"I'm pretty sure Dennis Brown is Denny."

"Denny?" Kate queried.

"Crewman on the RoseMarie."

* * *

"Are you sure we should be doing this?" Kate asked, breathless and having to speak up from the ten yards she was behind Callie as they raced along the sea front towards the net shops. "I mean, shouldn't we call the police?"

"And tell them what?" Callie stopped long enough for Kate to catch up with her before continuing. "That we think that Denny Brown is really David Howe and that he killed the real Dennis Brown a year ago and assumed his identity before returning to Hastings, signing on with the RoseMarie and beginning his plan for revenge?"

"Well, that would be a start, yes." Kate stopped and held onto her side. "Look, can we just wait a minute, please. I've got a stitch."

Callie stopped and walked back to her.

"If you – we – are right, then Denny has killed five people so far, and is more than likely planning on killing at least one more. Let me tell you, confronting him is not a good idea," said Kate. She sat on a wall, took off one of her high heeled shoes and rubbed her foot.

Callie had to admit she had a point. "I know that's what I said I thought had happened," she said, "but we don't know it's true, do we? I mean, we know he claims to be Dennis Brown, but we don't know that he actually switched identities, or that he's guilty of murder. I mean, maybe he really is who he claims to be."

"And has just worn extremely well? I mean did he look thirty in that photograph? You said yourself that he doesn't look it now, didn't you?"

"True, but it's sometimes hard to tell what age people are, particularly fishermen."

"Because they age prematurely, not because they look younger than they are."

"Anyway, we don't even know that he'll be here, he could be at home or in the pub."

"But what if he is here? Honestly, Callie, you need to call the police, let them deal with it."

"I can hear Steve now, asking how come Jack and Simon didn't realise Denny was David Howe before."

"Why would they? They won't have actually met him," Kate told her. "They won't even have seen his name on the paperwork, he was always just the claimant so why would they question Denny's word about who he was? Nobody else did, did they?"

Callie sat down beside her.

"You really do think that Denny could be him? David Howe? And that he could be behind all these killings?"

"Yes, yes, I do, and I don't think confronting him about it is a good idea. We need to go to the police. We need to go to Steve. Please."

Callie looked along the road to the fishing sheds.

"Okay. But not Steve. I can't face him and he will just put the phone down on me. He really can't take any more of me telling him what to do. I'll call Jayne."

They sat on a bench, watching the sheds and beach for signs of the RoseMarie and David, or Denny, while Callie called Jayne and explained their theory.

"Leave it with me," Jayne told her firmly. "I'll round up a couple of uniforms and see if we can find this bloke and bring him in for questioning, but it will take a little time. Meanwhile, don't go near him, okay? Even if you see him, Callie, don't confront him. Don't do anything. Do you understand?"

"Yes," Callie responded weakly, but Jayne and Kate could tell she might not necessarily comply.

"Why don't we go up to your flat?" Kate asked. "We'll be more comfortable there."

But Callie had spotted Sharon Porter walking along the pavement, pushing a buggy with arms outstretched to reach beyond her pregnant stomach and waddling slightly with the effort. Callie jumped up and went over to her.

"Hello, Sharon," she said, "how are things going?"

"Oh, it's you, Doctor," Sharon frowned slightly. "We're fine."

"Bet you can't wait until you've had the baby." Callie had bent down to see the toddler in the pushchair and didn't see Denny by the net shops nor register the crunch of footsteps on the shingle behind her. It wasn't until he crossed the road that she suddenly registered his presence.

"Hello, Sharon love, Doctor." Denny bent forward to kiss Sharon on the cheek. "You ready to go?" he asked the young mum as Callie straightened, unable to keep the shock from her face. "I said I'd go with Shaz for her hospital appointment." He seemed puzzled by Callie's reaction and then saw Kate behind her, watching them closely.

"Yes." Sharon's eyes were anxiously flitting from one to the other. "Denny's been a real help. I don't know what I'd have done without him."

"I'm happy to do it, and I'm sure everything's fine with the little one. He will be here before you know it." His attention shifted from the odd little group to a marked police car that was just pulling up behind Callie and Kate. "Come on love, the car's just over here. I'll take this one." He grabbed the pushchair from Sharon and started briskly walking towards the car park. There was no way Sharon could keep up in her condition, but she tried, in a mix of walking and jogging while also supporting her tummy that looked painfully uncomfortable.

"Sharon! Wait!" Callie called out, running after her. With a groan, Kate took off her shoes and tried to follow, but was making slow progress over the stones.

Callie turned and saw Jayne getting out of the police car. She pointed ahead in the direction that Denny had gone.

"He's got the baby!" she shouted before turning back to her pursuit, then saw that Sharon had stopped and was bending over, clutching her side. Callie was torn, did she run after the suspected murderer with the toddler in a pushchair? Or stay with the distressed pregnant mum? Seeing Jayne closing in on them and followed by the two uniformed officers, Abi Adeola and her colleague Joe from Mrs Caldwell's flat, Callie stopped and placed a hand on Sharon's back.

"It's okay, just try to breathe through it," she advised her, then turned and shouted to Jayne as she sprinted by with the two officers. "He went that way. He's got the toddler in a pushchair and I think he's got a car!"

Abi immediately turned and ran back towards the road and the police car, speaking into her radio, asking for back-up as she ran.

Sharon's contraction slowly dissipated and she began to straighten up, rubbing her belly.

"Okay?" Callie asked her.

"Yes, it was just, oof!" Her face contorted with pain as a second contraction started. Callie took out her phone and was calling for an ambulance as Kate arrived, grimacing as she hobbled over to them, her very unsuitable footwear in hand.

"Ouch, these pebbles are hell to walk on," she said. "Oh dear." She noticed Sharon's pain-filled face. "Is she?"

"Having a baby? Yes," Callie replied calmly.

"It's nothing, I was in labour eighteen hours last time," Sharon told Callie between pants. "Just make sure Tommy is okay."

"I'm sure he'll be fine," Callie said, trying to sound more positive than she was. "Denny won't hurt him, will he?"

Sharon was not in a position to reply, puffing as she was through another contraction.

"And this is a second baby, so it might come faster," Callie told her and Kate. "We'll stay with you until the ambulance gets here."

Kate didn't seem altogether happy with the idea.

They all watched as a car came hurtling from the car park, heading towards the road, just as the police car pulled forward blocking the exit. There was an almighty crash.

"Tommy!" Sharon screamed and tried to run towards the car before doubling over with another contraction.

"Abi!" Callie shouted and turned to Kate. "Stay with her!" And she ran towards the two cars.

Denny's car had driven straight into the police car, hitting the driver's door head on. Callie opened the rear doors of Denny's car first, checking to see if there was a toddler in there, but there was nothing but an empty child's seat. Where had he left Tommy? She looked over towards where she had left Sharon and Kate, and heaved a sigh of relief as she saw Jayne return, wheeling a pushchair with the screaming toddler. Joe was running as fast as he could back towards Callie and the cars. She would rely on him to deal with Denny, she decided, so with no more than a brief glance into Denny's car, to see the airbag slowly deflating, leaving him looking dazed and bleeding from a cut to his face, Callie went straight to the police car to help Abi.

The driver's side window of the police car had shattered, the door was badly dented and Callie feared the worst as she looked inside. The airbag had deflated and she could see Abi lying across the car, with the top half of her body on the passenger seat. She was breathing and seemed to be conscious.

"It's okay, Abi," Callie said. "Help is on the way."

It looked as if the fact that Abi had not had time to put on a seatbelt might have saved her life as she had been able to throw herself out of the way once she realised that Denny was going to crash into her. Largely out of the way – Abi's legs were still in the driver's footwell and there was blood coming from somewhere. Callie reached down to touch the leg, feeling for where the blood might be coming from, and trying to feel if there were any broken bones. Abi groaned.

"Sorry," Callie said and grunted herself as she tried to reach further in, but the bonnet of Denny's car, wedged as it was in the driver's door, was making it difficult so Callie went to the passenger side and opened the door.

"It's okay, don't move, an ambulance is on the way, but I just need to examine you and see if we can stop the bleeding."

Abi nodded weakly and looked as if she was going to pass out.

"Stay with me, okay?" Callie reached forward, felt gently down her leg and pulled the badly torn trousers slightly to the side allowing her to see the broken edge of tibia poking out and blood pulsing from the wound. She turned and saw Joe had arrived behind her and was watching, anxiety etched across his face.

"I'm going to need a belt or a tie," she said, "something I can use as a tourniquet."

The man quickly started to pull his belt from his trousers.

"And we're going to need more ambulances" – she looked at the two cars so tightly melded together – "and the fire brigade." He nodded and, handing over his belt, picked up his radio. It would do him good to keep busy, she thought as she gently eased the belt around Abi's leg and tightened it, pleased to see the blood flow slow.

"What can I do?" Gauri and others had run out from the surgery to help.

"I think that lady over there is about to give birth," she told her colleague, nodding towards Sharon, who was now on her back, knees bent, and grunting as she pushed. Kate was holding her coat as a screen to shield her as much as possible, and trying not to look at what was happening. The toddler was still screaming as Gauri hurried over, but the new baby was out and adding to the noise levels before she got there.

The practice nurse came over to help Callie. She had sensibly thought to bring some sterile dressing packs and opened them for Callie to cover Abi's gaping leg wound.

There was a shout of anger and pain from Denny's car as he regained consciousness and tried to free himself, but Abi's colleague, Joe had thought to cuff Denny to the steering wheel. He wasn't going anywhere.

Callie turned back to her priority patient.

"Are you injured anywhere else, Abi?" she asked.

"I don't think so," she said weakly.

Callie was relieved to hear sirens as the first of the emergency responders began to arrive. Her job now was to direct them to the most seriously injured, in this case Abi. She was pretty sure they would need the fire brigade to help extricate her. She looked over to where Gauri seemed to be dealing with the new baby and the aftermath of the delivery perfectly well, and breathed a sigh of relief. One less thing to worry about, but it was still going to be a long process to deal with everything.

"What the fuck happened?"

She turned to see Miller and Jeffries looking at the chaos. It was going to a *very* long process, she corrected herself. And, as she wiped the blood from her hands and debated what she was going to reply, she was relieved to see Jayne hurrying over and throwing her a look that told Callie to stay out of it. With a nod, Callie chose to go over and see Sharon instead.

Sharon was sitting up now, with a surgery blanket covering her lower half and clutching a baby to her breast.

"It's a girl!" she said, adoration written all over her face.

Gauri released the toddler from his pushchair and brought him over to see his mother.

"Come on, meet your little sister," she said and the boy came and sat by his mum, tears drying on his face as she hugged him and showed him the baby.

"Isn't she beautiful?" she said.

The boy looked a little unsure. Callie could understand that — newborn babies do not, generally, look overly attractive with blood and vernix covering them, but she was clearly beautiful to her mum. Callie wondered if she would ever look with such adoration at a baby of her own.

"How's Denny?" Sharon asked, looking up and jerking her from her reverie. "Is he okay?"

"He'll live," Callie told her, resisting the urge to find out if Sharon knew anything about what he had been doing the last few weeks. She hoped not. She didn't want to think the young mum had colluded in the murder of her husband and all the others. Didn't want to worry about what would happen to the children if she turned out to have been involved in it all and was sent to prison, so she went over to Kate who was sitting a short distance away, looking a bit green about the gills.

"How are you doing?" she asked.

"Oh my God, I am never, ever having children," Kate said. "That was absolutely hideous."

Chapter 32

Callie watched as the firemen carefully cut Abi and Denny out of the wreckage of the two cars. Abi was taken to her ambulance on a stretcher, while Denny was able to walk himself, albeit handcuffed to a police officer. She was pretty sure he would be quickly transferred to the police station once the cut to his head had been stitched and dressed. Having made sure all the injured along with Shaz, Tommy and the new baby were on their way to hospital, Callie took Kate up to her flat where they could watch what was happening below from the comfort of her balcony.

The sun was going down but the road was still sealed off to normal traffic, yet Kate disappeared downstairs and magicked a bottle of wine from somewhere. Perhaps Linda kept a bottle in her office for special occasions or emergency use, Callie thought as she leant over the balcony, glass in hand and watched as the last car was winched onto a low-loader. Miller had not spoken to her, not even while they were both at the scene, although, to be fair, she hadn't spoken to him either. He had left as soon as he reasonably could and she had been relieved to see him go. She had well and truly burnt her bridges there, she thought, but strangely, she didn't feel sad about. She was more concerned about what would happen to her role as a police doctor, which said a lot about her relationship with him.

"Talk to me," Kate said.

"I think I'm going to have to resign from my police role."

"Do you think Steve is going to put in a complaint about you?"

"I don't think it matters. We can't work together, not without someone like Jayne to act as go-between, and that's not fair on anyone."

"And you can't see you two getting back together?"

Callie shook her head emphatically.

"Seeing Billy, kissing him, changed everything. I didn't feel the same about Steve after that."

"You said you felt like you had cheated on him."

"I was wrong, I realised that what I actually felt was that I had been cheating on Billy all this time."

"Maybe getting him back for his affair?"

"Maybe, subconsciously, that was a factor, but I think Steve was an itch I needed to scratch. You know" – she turned to look at Kate – "he made my stomach flip whenever he smiled at me and had this glint in his eye, and I thought I wanted to sink into his arms and let him protect me, but in the end, my stomach stopped reacting and I found his protection claustrophobic."

"You have always needed to be in control."

"And much as Steve thought he wanted an opinionated woman, he really didn't want a control freak. The relationship was doomed from the start."

"I can see that," Kate said. "So what are you going to do about it?"

Callie laughed. "Well, I don't think I have to end it with Steve, because I'm pretty sure he's got in there first."

"About Billy, I meant."

"I'm going to take it slowly, see if he wants me back."

"I'm pretty sure that's a given."

"I hope so," Callie said, but she didn't look sure.

"Do you think he'll come back to Hastings?"

"No. Matt said he has been offered the permanent position in Brighton and I think he should take that." She turned to Kate. "Maybe it's time for a change. And Brighton's not so far away, not as far as Belfast anyway. I might even look for a job nearer to there, if he wants me to do that."

"I have no doubt that he will. You've always been the love of his life. He just had a moment of madness."

"Several weeks of madness," Callie corrected her.

"But is that worth breaking up a good partnership?"

Callie didn't answer.

The doorbell rang.

"Speak of the devil," Kate said with a smile and Callie shook her head. It wouldn't be Billy, would it?

But there he was on the video screen, waving a bottle of wine.

"Thought you might need a top-up," he said as she pressed the buzzer to let him in. "I heard that you've had a busy day." He nodded at Kate who, Callie was sure, had let him know.

They talked him through the events and not long after they had finished, Jayne arrived, with another bottle, which was just as well as they had finished the first two by then.

"So, come on, Jayne," Billy encouraged her. "What's been happening? Tell us all."

"How's Abi for a start?" Callie added.

"Abi is doing well, they've operated on her leg and the surgeons are happy."

Callie was relieved and let Jayne carry on with her news. Initial DNA comparisons had been done with the paperwork from solicitors, relating to the case when David Howe contested the will. There had been a verbal report from the lab saying that David Howe's DNA matched Denny's and that it was definitely Carl's DNA that had been submitted in the original case, not his older brother Simon's. There was no doubt that, as a young boy, Carl had assisted his family in shutting out David – or Denny, as Callie couldn't help but think of him. He had a good case for fraud, although whether or not he would have got anything if he had contested the will was another matter. Just bringing the case would have cost the family dear, in legal fees if nothing else, and they could have lost everything – the boat, the house, their futures. So they had connived to stop him, once and for all. They could never have predicted that he would return and wreak such a terrible revenge.

"Denny has been discharged from hospital and arrested for murder. He'll be interviewed tomorrow and meanwhile we have to pull together all the evidence for the CPS to consider charges," Jayne said.

"Do you think you'll have enough if he doesn't confess?" Callie asked.

Jayne shrugged. "That's a good question, but I'm pretty sure we will get a custody extension to give us more time to investigate given the seriousness of the crimes."

"Will you be looking again at the real Dennis Brown's death?" Kate asked.

"We will, but it will be difficult to find any evidence this late in the day, and who knows, perhaps it was an accident and he only thought about swapping names after the event."

Somehow, Callie didn't think so. She was pretty sure poor Dennis Brown was the first victim.

"Oh, and," Jayne continued, "I checked the records and Ms Howe, Denny's mother, killed herself after the claim got chucked out."

"Don't tell me she hanged herself?" Callie said.

"She did, yes. I read the coroner's report and it seems Harry Hudson was a bit of a bastard and never acknowledged the boy. When he died, she'd pinned her hopes on finally getting recognition for her son, and when the claim fell apart and she was made out to be some kind of fantasist, she couldn't take it."

Suddenly everything was falling into place. Denny's mother had always said Harry Hudson was the father and to have the court say he wasn't, and with all the gossip and Rose Hudson's accusations that the father could be anyone, must have tipped her over the edge. It was a sad story and explained why Denny had chosen the hanging theme. He blamed them all for his mother's suicide and he was making sure that their deaths were a punishment that fitted the crime he felt they had committed.

"Does Carl know Denny's been arrested?"

"Yes, and he was mightily relieved to be off the hook, even if we can't bring his family back."

Callie could believe it.

"And what about Sharon? Did she know anything about what Denny was doing?" she asked Jayne.

"We haven't been able to interview her yet," she said. "I mean, she's just got home with a new baby, and we need to be a little circumspect, but we've put a new family liaison officer in with her, seeing as Abi will be in hospital for a while." Jayne looked a little uncomfortable. "She's a motherly type and I'm hoping Sharon will open up to her. She has already admitted she has been seeing Denny for a while, from even before her husband was killed. She said the marriage had been going through a rough patch but" – Jayne shrugged – "I'm not sure that would be enough."

"No, but you can see the attraction from Denny's point of view. First, he takes Simon's wife from him, then his life, his boat, his house… everything he thought he should have had in the first place and more." She looked into her wine for a moment. "But I agree. I can't believe Sharon knew he was behind all the deaths. Not her husband, surely?"

"We'll see. Time will tell and all that, but I think you are probably right. I can't see her wanting to get together with a man who had no compunction about killing anyone in his way. She'd always wonder if she was going to be next."

They finished the wine, and Kate made some excuse about needing to get back and do some packing. She tried to hint that Jayne should leave with her but Jayne was falling asleep in the armchair. In the end, Kate had to practically drag her out of the door, finally leaving Billy and Callie alone.

"That was subtle." He laughed as he turned back to Callie and moved a little closer. "I've accepted the permanent post in Brighton," he told her.

"Good," she replied and tilted her head up to his.

"Brighton's not so far," he said, his voice husky and his lips brushing hers.

"No," she agreed and kissed him. "I think I'd like it there."

THE END

If you enjoyed this book, please let others know by leaving a quick review on Amazon. Also, if you spot anything untoward in the paperback, get in touch. We strive for the best quality and appreciate reader feedback.

editor@thebookfolks.com

www.thebookfolks.com

BODY HEAT – Book 2

A series of deadly arson attacks piques the curiosity of Hastings police doctor Callie Hughes. Faced with police incompetence, once again she tries to find the killer herself, but her meddling won't win her any favours and in fact puts her in a compromising position.

GUILTY PARTY – Book 3

A lawyer in a twist at his home. Another dead in a private pool. Someone has targeted powerful individuals in the coastal town of Hastings. Dr Callie Hughes uses her medical expertise to find the guilty party.

VITAL SIGNS – Book 4

When bodies of migrants begin to wash up on the Sussex coast, police doctor Callie Hughes has the unenviable task of inspecting them. But one body stands out to her as different. Convinced that finding the victim's identity will help crack the people smuggling ring, she decides to start her own investigation.

DEADLY REMEDIES – Book 5

When two elderly individuals pass away, it is not an unusual occurrence for seaside town doctor and medical examiner Callie Hughes. But she notices that both of the deceased had a suitcase packed, and her suspicions are aroused. Who is the killer that is prematurely taking them to their final destination?

MURDER LUST – Book 6

After noticing strange marks on the body of a woman found dead in a holiday let, police doctor Callie Hughes probes further. The police take her concerns about a serial killer seriously, but achieve little when another body if found. Callie is possibly the only obstacle to the murderer getting away with the crime, and that makes her a potential target.

BONES OF CONTENTION – Book 7

Work on a new patio in the garden of a house in an English seaside town stops abruptly when bones are discovered. Police doctor Callie Hughes is called in to confirm the remains are human. Her curiosity is aroused but her sleuthing is hampered by a stalker whose obsession with her is quickly escalating.

CRIMES OF THE FALLEN
by James Andrew

When DI John Belivat is called to the scene of a murdered
woman, left naked on the seafront of a Scottish town, it
brings back all his fears about the fate of his own missing
daughter. He focuses on the victim, trying to establish her
identity. But only after another body is found will the
detective be able to piece together a motive and find a killer.

*Sign up to our mailing list to find out about new releases
and special offers!*

www.thebookfolks.com